The Happy Hollisters and the Punch and Judy Mystery

By JERRY WEST

Illustrated by Helen S. Hamilton

DOUBLEDAY & COMPANY, INC.

GARDEN CITY, NEW YORK

Contents

CHAPTER 1

WHACK, WHACK!

"COME one, come all!" cried Pete Hollister. "The great Punch and Judy show is about to start!"

Pete, twelve, and oldest of the five Hollisters, stood in the middle of the lawn beside a red booth. It was a foot higher than his blond crew-cut head, and the puppet stage was covered with a black shade.

A handful of children fidgeted in front of the booth. Dark-haired Sue Hollister, four, jumped up and down and tugged at the hand of her sister Holly, who was six. She, in turn, wrinkled her nose, tossed her pigtails and called out, "Ricky, stop galloping around!"

Her red-haired, freckle-faced brother, a year older, did not answer, but slapped himself like a horse once more, somersaulted on the grass and landed at Holly's feet. This made Ann Hunter laugh, while her younger brother, Jeff, grinned and little Donna Martin looked on shyly.

Pete spoke to a tall boy with straight tousled hair. "Are all the pennies collected, Dave?"

Dave Mead nodded and jiggled the coins in a tin

can. He was twelve, too, and Pete's best friend. He looked around the Hollisters' back yard and said, "I don't see Joey and Will. They told me they'd come."

"And what about Pam?" Curly-haired Ann asked anxiously. "We can't begin without all the Hollisters."

"Pam!" the children chorused.

"Where are you?" Ricky shouted.

It was ten-year-old Pam who had thought up the Punch and Judy show to raise money for a special project. This was the Fifty Fund, sponsored by the Shoreham newspaper to send fifty needy children to summer camp.

Then Pete had hit on the idea of earning fifty pounds of pennies. He had weighed coins and found that there were one hundred forty-seven pennies in a pound. Pam's speedy arithmetic showed that fifty pounds of them would equal seventy-three dollars and fifty cents, enough to give one boy or girl two weeks in camp.

For two weeks the Hollisters' spacious, rambling home on the shore of Pine Lake had been busy with the Punch and Judy preparations. First Pam had borrowed a book of instructions from the library. Using it, the children had carved and painted the wooden faces, dressed the little hand puppets in gay costumes and constructed the stage.

Now everything was set for the first show. The neighborhood children had arrived on the Hollisters' lawn, and Pete, as the showman, had already

6

fitted one of the puppets over each of his hands.

Punch, with his big curved nose and chin and a roguish grin, was ready to perform on Pete's right hand. On his left was a long-snouted dragon.

"Hurry, Pam! Where are you?" Holly called impatiently.

"I'll go find her," Ann Hunter volunteered. She was Pam's age, and had black hair which hung in ringlets. Her gray eyes danced with excitement and her dimples showed as she ran off to look for her best friend.

"Oh there you are!" cried Ann as she spied Pam standing next to the mailbox which stood in the shrubbery along the sidewalk. "The show can't start without you!"

"I'll be there in a minute," Pam promised, then added, "I wish Mr. Barnes would hurry! He's late with the mail today."

"You must be expecting an important letter," Ann said with a sidewise look at her friend.

"Oh no, it's not from a boy if that's what you mean," Pam said with a shake of her fluffy golden hair. Then her brown eyes sparkled and she lowered her voice. "I'll let you in on a secret, but you mustn't tell anyone."

As Ann promised, a twig snapped in the bushes behind the girls, but they were too busy talking to notice the noise. Pam confided that she had entered an essay contest about a children's book called *The Mystery in Venice*.

Winners were to be announced shortly.

"And guess what, Ann! First prize is a trip for two around the world!" As her friend's eyes widened, Pam explained that the second prize was a trip to Hawaii and the third prize a real palomino horse.

"I can hardly wait to hear," said Pam. "But I guess I'll just have to be patient," she added with a sigh, and the two girls ran toward the Punch and Judy show.

As they disappeared around the house, the bushes moved and two heads came out. Joey Brill and his friend Will Wilson stood up. Joey was Pete's age but larger. Will was big, too, and always tagged after Joey. Both of them delighted in annoying smaller children and making trouble for the Hollisters.

"Do you want to see the show?" Joey asked. "We were invited."

"No, it'll probably be crummy," Will said.

"Then I know how to make some excitement," Joey said. He whispered to his companion, and the pair crept off through the foliage, working their way unseen toward the back of the Hollisters' garage.

On the lawn, Pam announced the show, and Pete stepped into the back of the red booth. The black shade popped up. Punch stuck his saucy head over the edge of the stage and in a high falsetto voice said,

"La-dies and gentlemen. What a beautiful day to take a walk along the shore of Pine Lake. Roo-to-to! Roo-to-to-it!"

8

Punch strutted back and forth, bobbing his head and shaking his tall green hat as the onlookers giggled. "I used to be a tightrope walker once in the circus," Punch said. "I'll see how close I can come to the shore without falling in!"

The puppet wagged this way and that, all the time singing, "Roo-to-to-to-to-it!" Finally he fell into the imaginary lake. Pete shouted, "Splash!" and Punch popped up again at once.

"Help me! Save me!" he cried out. "I just remembered, I can't swim!"

With that, up from the water came the long snout of the green dragon, as Pete deftly manipulated it.

"Ow!" Punch cried. "I'm a goner for sure! If I don't drown, the monster will eat me!"

"Eat you!" the funny-looking creature replied. "Who wants to eat an old wooden-head like you? Why your nose alone is enough to scare small babies."

"Don't talk about my pretty nose. Glub! Glub!" Punch said, going out of sight for a moment.

The monster turned to the audience. "Shall I save him?"

"Yes!" the children shouted.

"Hurry!" piped little Sue loudly. The dragon grabbed Punch's hat in his mouth and pulled him back onto the stage.

"There now, Mr. Punch, you're all right, aren't you?" the monster asked, his big jaws moving up and down.

"Yes, but I'm all wet," Punch complained, shaking himself. "You got me wetter than I would have been."

"How's that?" the monster asked, looking perplexed.

"I'll show you," Punch said in his squeaky voice, "if you'll look yonder over the lake."

As the unwary creature turned his head, Punch disappeared and came up with a stick. *Whack!* *Whack!* He hit the long green snout. "Take that, and that, for getting me wetter than I would have been!" Punch shouted gleefully.

Just then the youngsters, who were looking on enthralled, became aware of another noise. From behind the puppet stage Joey Brill and Will Wilson came racing across the lawn toward the audience. They ran about ten feet apart, holding a clothesline between them.

"Stop!" Pam cried out, "Or else you'll hit—" Before she had a chance to finish her sentence, the bullies knocked the Punch and Judy booth flat! Pete was thrown to the ground as the rope caught him behind the shoulders. Punch went flying in one direction, the monster in another.

The neighborhood children were stunned for a moment as Joey and Will dropped the rope and sped off as fast as their legs could carry them.

"Oh you!" Holly cried, stamping her foot. "Joey, you're meaner than Punch."

Ricky raced after them, but the two bullies outdistanced him. He returned red-faced with anger.

"Stop!"

"That Joey Brill better watch out," he declared. "He's going to be sorry!"

By this time Pete had untangled himself from the booth.

"Are you all right?" Pam asked her brother. Pete rubbed a bump on his forehead ruefully. "I guess I am," he said. "Where's Zip?"

"Here, Zip!" he called out. The Hollisters' beautiful collie dog jumped from a clump of cattails growing along the shore not far from the Hollisters' house. He bounded across the yard and circled around Pete, bobbing his head and whining.

"I want you to keep a lookout for Joey and Will," Pete told the dog. "Don't let them come in the yard while we're putting on our show."

Zip barked sharply three times, walked over to the side of the driveway and lay down in the grass with his head between his forepaws.

"Now we can go on with the show in peace," Pete declared. "Do we still have our money?" he called out to Dave Mead. His friend jiggled the tin can, making the pennies jump up and down. "It's not fifty pounds," Dave said, "but at least it's a start." Then he added, "Look, here come more customers."

Across the lawn walked two women and a small girl. With a squeal of excitement Ann Hunter jumped up. "It's my mother! Our company came!" She raced toward them.

The woman and the girl with Mrs. Hunter both were very pretty, with jet black hair, gray eyes and fair complexions. After Ann had greeted them, she led the way over to her playmates.

"I would like you to meet Mrs. Boschi and her daughter Nada," Ann said. "They're from Italy and are going to stay with us a few days before they return." Mrs. Hunter explained that Mrs. Boschi was a famous dress designer who was in this country on business. Pam said they were glad to meet the visitors and asked Nada how old she was.

"I am nine years," replied the Italian girl, saying the words carefully. Her glossy hair was straight and cut in bangs.

"Where's her father?" Holly whispered to Ann.

The older girl bent close to Holly's ear. "He's not living," she answered.

Just then Ricky spoke up. "We're having a Punch and Judy show," he said. "You want to see it?" He pointed to the booth which Pete and Dave had readied again.

But when the little visitor looked up at the puppet stage she burst into tears.

"Oh my goodness," Pam said worried. "What's the matter, Nada?"

CHAPTER 2

AN UNLUCKY LOOKOUT

As THE youngsters looked on, surprised, Mrs. Boschi took a handkerchief from her purse and wiped the tears from Nada's eyes.

Then the little girl told why she had cried. Her great-uncle, Giovanni Boschi, was an expert Pulcinella showman.

"Pulcinella is Punch's Italian name," Nada's mother put in quickly. Her daughter went on to say that four weeks before, Uncle Giovanni had mysteriously disappeared.

"Oh dear," said Pam. "No wonder you cried, Nada."

"But Italy is such a small country," Ricky spoke up. "Why can't they find him?"

Nada told the Hollisters about the mountains and lakes and rugged coastline of her homeland.

"It's not big," she said, "but there are many good places to hide people." Then she brightened and smiled. "I have a hundred lire," she said. "May I see your show?"

"Yikes, that's a lot of money!" Ricky exclaimed.

"It's only sixteen cents," Mrs. Boschi told him

with a smile, as she and Nada dropped some foreign coins into the tin can held by Dave.

Mrs. Hunter also stayed to enjoy the show, which got under way again in a few minutes.

Before Pete entered the booth he told the audience that he and Pam had made one puppet which had no name yet. He held up the stout figure with red, bulging cheeks and a purple nose. "I'm going to call him Joey," announced Pete. As the onlookers laughed, he ducked into the booth. The curtain went up. Punch and the new puppet sprang upon the stage.

"So you're Joey who ruined my show!" Punch said in his high, reedy voice.

"Yes, I'm the one. I was just having some fun."

"Oh, it's fun you want?" Punch disappeared, and once again returned with a stick held between his hands. "I know a game that's a lot of fun," he went on.

"Show me," the other demanded.

Punch took a swing and Joey ducked. He swung again and Joey dodged.

"Stop, you'll hurt me!" the red-faced puppet cried out.

"Don't complain. I haven't hit you yet," Punch replied impishly. "Hold still, and I'll show you how much fun it is to get whacked."

"I won't!"

"You will!"

Then Punch said, "Turn around. Here comes

15

your friend Will." When Joey turned, Punch whacked him. "There, take that, and that!"

Joey disappeared. As Punch laughed loudly, a puppet with a yellow face, red body, horns and a tail popped up behind him. Punch turned around and stopped laughing.

"Whoa-oa-oa!" he quavered. "Who—who are you?"

"The devil."

"Well, go away. I don't like devils," Punch declared, bobbing his head demandingly.

"I'm going to take you," the horned puppet said, "for being so mean to a sweet boy like Joey." The devil pounced, Punch howled and the two dropped out of sight.

As the children laughed and clapped gleefully, the curtain went down.

"That was a very good show," Nada said.

"And we collected a dollar forty cents," Dave spoke up, "just about one pound of pennies."

While Pete, Ricky and Dave carried the puppet stage into the Hollisters' garage, the girls plied Nada with more questions about the mystery of the missing Giovanni. They learned that he was a retired merchant. Pulcinella had been his hobby for years. He made very interesting painted faces, especially on Punch.

"You can tell one of Uncle Giovanni's Punch faces because there is a mole on his nose," Nada said.

"On your uncle's nose?" Sue piped up.

"Oh no," the girl replied, laughing. "The puppet's."

Nada's great-uncle had traveled around Italy putting on shows because he liked children. He had a collapsible stage which he carried on the back of his motorcycle.

Now the boys returned and listened intently as the little Italian girl continued. Her uncle's booth and puppets had been abandoned in a park in Milan. His motorcycle had been found wrecked on the big highway. "We looked in hospitals and everywhere," the dark-haired child told them, "but we could not find him."

"Too bad we're not Italians," Holly said, "or we could help you."

"Thank you anyway," Nada replied. Then she ran to her mother, who was leaving with Mrs. Hunter. Ann started to follow, then darted back and whispered in Pam's ear, "I hope you win a prize!"

"Don't forget that's our secret," Pam said as Ann skipped off.

After lunch, all the Hollisters but Sue went to the garage and took turns practicing with the puppets. Pam liked the part of Punch's wife and played it in a high squeaky voice. She acted the baby well, too, imitating his crying better than any of the others.

"Pete, you and Pam ought to do the show," Holly said, "'cause you're best." Ricky agreed.

"I wish we could get a crowd to see it," Pam said, switching to her own low voice.

17

"Maybe Mother can give us a good idea," Holly said. The children left the garage and trooped across the yard to the kitchen door, where they were met by a delightful aroma of baking cookies. As they entered, Mrs. Hollister, a pretty and slender woman, was pulling a tin sheet of gingersnaps from the oven. She set it on the table, wiped her hands on her apron and with a spatula slid several of the cookies onto a plate. "Help yourselves," she said smiling.

"Mmmm, they're good warm," Ricky declared, and in the same breath added, "Mother, we need a big audience for our show if we're going to collect fifty pounds of pennies."

"Do you know how we can make money fast?" Pete asked, reaching for a second cookie.

"Daddy's committee of the Rotary Club is meeting here tonight," Mrs. Hollister said. "Why don't you ask them?"

"Maybe we can put on Punch and Judy for them!" Pam suggested.

"Ricky!" Mrs. Hollister said. "That's enough cookies now. There won't be any left for the men this evening."

After supper, Pam helped her mother ready the house. They finished only a few minutes before the committee members began to arrive. Mr. Hollister held the meeting on their large open porch. The children hovered in the front yard, making certain not to disturb their father's guests.

But when business was over and refreshments

were served, Pete called out, "Is it all right now, Dad?" Mr. Hollister, a tall, handsome, athletic-looking man, nodded to his son, and the children trooped up onto the porch. Pete stepped forward.

"Gentlemen," he said seriously, "we're raising money for the summer camp fund and would like to put on a Punch and Judy show for you. The price is as many pennies as you would like to give."

"Splendid idea," said Mr. Thompson, the Rotary treasurer. "Why don't you stage it tomorrow noon in the park in the Town Square. Our club meets in a restaurant across from there and all the men will come to see the play."

"Maybe a lot of other people too," Mr. Hollister added.

"Oh, great!" Ricky exclaimed. "I'll be the barker!"

There was a buzz of excitement as the men discussed the project. All seemed certain that it would attract a large crowd.

"Maybe we could put an announcement in the newspaper," Pam said.

"Good idea," was her father's reply. "Do it by telephone right away and it will appear tomorrow morning."

"Tell the paper the Rotary Club is sponsoring you," Mr. Thompson instructed.

Pam hastened into the house and soon came out again.

"The editor promised to put the notice on page one," she reported.

Since it was not yet dark, the girls ran over to the Hunters' house to tell their playmates the big news. Pete picked up Dave Mead and followed them. All the children wanted to help in the project. Nada offered to set up a lemonade booth with Ann.

"Swell idea, Nada!" Pete said. "We may be able to earn all of our money in one day!"

The Hollisters went to bed that night full of exciting ideas. But there was one thought uppermost in Pam's mind. Would Mr. Barnes, the postman, bring her a letter telling that she had won a prize?

Next morning the children practiced their puppetry. After an hour, Pam went over to Ann's house to help make the lemonade. Then she returned to her own postbox and waited for Mr. Barnes. He arrived with a handful of letters which Pam took eagerly. She looked at one after another. None for her.

"Oh dear," she said, and walked slowly toward the house.

Shortly before noon, Dave, Ann and Nada came over. A few minutes later a pickup truck arrived from The Trading Post. This was a combination hardware, toy and sporting-goods shop which Mr. Hollister operated in the center of town. Driving the truck was Indy Roades, a good-natured Indian from New Mexico, who worked for Mr. Hollister.

"Hi, Indy!" Ricky called out. "Everything's ready. Let's load it on."

The Punch and Judy booth, the puppets, a long table for the lemonade, a large checkered tablecloth, Sue's baby scale, some brown paper bags and a big carton were put in the truck with other paraphernalia. Then the children climbed in, followed by Zip, and Indy drove to the park in the Town Square. There, the mayor himself awaited them.

"I saw the notice in this morning's paper," he said, "and wish to congratulate you on your efforts to aid the Fifty Fund."

Pete and Pam shook hands with the mayor, then quickly began preparing their Punch and Judy booth. Dave, Ricky and the others helped set up the lemonade table.

As they did, Holly called Ricky aside and whispered, "I want to keep a lookout for Joey and Will. If they come along this time we'll be ready for them." She pointed to a tree nearby.

Ricky gave his sister a boost and she shinned to the first stout branch, then climbed out on it. Before her eyes, cradled in some branches, was a robin's nest. In it were three beautiful blue eggs.

"Oh dear," Holly said to herself, "I'd better get off this limb before I shake the eggs out of the nest." She began to crawl back but the branch shook. Then she decided to hang by her hands and swing along the limb. Holly dropped down, but the branch was too fat for her to grasp, and one hand slipped off.

"Help!" she screeched, hanging by one arm. Ricky immediately snatched the checkered tablecloth and called to Pete, "Come on, quick! We'll catch her in this!"

The two boys had barely stretched the tablecloth

beneath their frantic sister when down she came! Holly landed so hard that Pete and Ricky tumbled to the ground. But the girl was not hurt, for the tablecloth had broken her fall.

The three picked themselves up and went over to the large crowd which had collected to see what was going on.

Ricky stood to one side with Dave and went into his pitchman's act.

"Hurry, hurry, hurry! It's the greatest Punch and Judy show on earth!" he cried out. "Come see Punch and the dragon! Mrs. Judy and the baby, too!"

The noonday crowd, laughing good-naturedly, began to drop their pennies into Dave's tin can. There were so many that the can overflowed time after time, and the boy emptied the coins into the large carton the puppeteers had brought along for that purpose. Meanwhile, Nada and Ann did a booming lemonade business as the hot sun made everyone thirsty.

"Come on, Pam," Pete said to his sister. "Let's begin."

Up went the shade, and Punch appeared.

"Judy, my Judy, where are you?" Punch called out in his high-pitched voice.

"I'm down here with the baby," squeaked Pam.

"Well, come on up. I want to see you."

"But I must feed our baby."

"Bring him along too."

22

Down she came!

Immediately Mrs. Punch appeared, holding her infant. He looked just like Judy, only smaller.

"See, see what I mean!" Punch exclaimed, addressing the audience. "Isn't that a beautiful baby? Looks just like me."

The little puppet reached from his mother's arms and grabbed Punch by the nose as the crowd laughed.

"Hey, stop that!" Punch said. "You're hurting my beautiful nose."

"Waaah, waah!" went the baby.

"Stop that, I say," Punch ordered, shaking the infant.

"You're hurting my child!" came Pam's falsetto voice.

"Call him off!" Punch demanded, as the baby grabbed his nose again. "Well, there's one way to get rid of him!" Punch cried out. He flung the infant to the ground. The onlookers gasped at the scoundrel's actions. But instantly, Zip, the Hollisters' collie dog, leaped forward, grabbed Judy's baby and ran off across the square.

CHAPTER 3

A CLUE FROM ITALY

"Zip! Come back with Baby Punch!" Holly shouted, as she and Ricky dashed like whippets after the fleeing collie.

The dog raced around the booth, with no one able to put a hand on him. Then he jumped into a clump of bushes at the side of the park.

"Come out of there!" Ricky called sternly to the dog. The youngsters heard several barks. But instead of Zip appearing, out scrambled Joey and Will on hands and knees!

"What were you doing in there?" Holly asked in surprise. Joey said nothing, but sauntered off, with Will tagging behind him.

The pursuers had no more time for questions, because Zip darted from the other side of the shrubbery. Suddenly he was joined by a big black dog who tried to nip at Baby Punch.

Zip dropped Baby Punch on the grass and growled at the intruder. Then the black dog lunged at the puppet, but Zip snatched the doll away in time and streaked around the park. The black dog tried to follow, but soon gave up and wandered off again.

Now the chase grew to be a merry one. The onlookers reached down and tried to grab Zip as he zigzagged among them, holding the limp puppet between his teeth.

"Officer Cal! Help us catch our naughty dog!" Holly called out to a young policeman, who was driving past in a squad car. The handsome officer, who knew the Hollisters well, parked near by and joined in the chase. But Zip was like a greased lightning bolt as he dashed about enjoying himself thoroughly.

Finally the collie bounded toward Sue on his umpteenth turn around the green. The little girl said, "Please stand still, Zip, so I can catch you."

The dog stopped instantly, and dropped the puppet at the child's feet. The onlookers cheered and clapped.

"Thank you, Zip," said Sue. As the collie wagged his tail, she returned Baby Punch to the puppet show.

Instead of hurting the performance, the commotion brought more spectators and pennies continued to drop into the tin can with a cheery clink.

The show went on, with Mr. Punch getting what he deserved for the ill treatment of his baby. Laughter filled the Town Square as children and grownups alike chuckled at the excellent performance.

When it was over, Ricky immediately began to weigh the pennies on Sue's baby scale. He scooped

"Please stand still!"

up handfuls of coppers and put them into a paper bag until the needle of the scale pointed to ten pounds. Four bags were filled in this manner. "Yikes! Look, everybody!" Ricky shouted as he measured out the fifth ten-pound batch of coins.

"We've made it!" Pete said happily. "Crickets! Fifty pounds of pennies!"

Amid congratulations from passersby, somebody said to Pete, "Did I hear you correctly?" The boy turned to see a young man with a newspaper under one arm. He introduced himself as Ken Speed, a reporter from the Shoreham *Times*.

"Yes, we've made our goal," Pam said proudly.

"Good," the reporter replied. "My paper did all it could to help your show." He unfolded the newspaper and pointed to an article on the first page which told about the Punch and Judy performance.

"No wonder we had so many people here," Pam said. "Thank you very much, Mr. Speed. We plan to take the money to your newspaper this afternoon."

"Fine. And when you do, stop by to see me. I'd like some more information about your Punch and Judy project."

As they spoke, Nada leaned forward to read the story. Suddenly she gasped in surprise. "Oh Pam, look!" she exclaimed.

The Italian girl pointed to an article beneath the Punch and Judy story. Its dateline said "Florence, Italy," and Nada read it aloud.

"Search for Giovanni Boschi, famous Pulcinella

artist, was given new hope today as authentic Boschi puppets appeared for sale in Florence."

"Who's Florence?" Ricky asked, half listening. "Your sister?"

Pam explained that Florence is a name of a city in Italy.

"We Italians call it Firenze," said Nada.

"The puppets are a wonderful clue!" Pam exclaimed. "Perhaps you'll find your uncle very soon."

Nada said she could hardly wait to return to Italy to help in the search. "But Mother has to stop in Paris first," she added. "I hope we don't stay there too long."

While the girls were packing the puppets in the box, the boys helped Indy load the Punch and Judy stage on the truck. They were too busy to notice Joey and Will walking casually up to where the five bags of pennies were neatly stacked beside the scale.

Will hung back a little distance. Joey bent down and picked up one of the heavy bags. As he did, Pete glimpsed him out of the corner of his eye and ran toward the troublemaker.

"Joey—!" Pete started to say, but was interrupted by a tall, portly man with a shock of white hair. With a big smile the man took the bag away from Joey.

"Thank you so much," the newcomer said jovially. He placed a hand on Joey's shoulder and called him one of Shoreham's most helpful youngsters.

The bully's mouth fell open and he looked up in disbelief.

"I assume," the tall man said, "that you are one of the Punch and Judy company."

Joey could only shake his head no, and Pete put his hand over his mouth to stifle a grin.

The man continued, "My name is Mr. Rader, and I am here to invite the Punch and Judy show people to have lunch with us at Rotary today."

"Crickets, that'll be great!" Pete called the other children over, and Mr. Rader repeated his invitation.

As the puppeteers beamed and accepted, Joey scowled, still held firmly by the large hand on his shoulder.

After Pete, Ricky, Pam, Nada and Dave each had lifted one of the sacks of pennies, Mr. Rader released Joey, who scuffed off, still scowling.

"This way, right across the street," their host said, and led the happy children to an air-conditioned restaurant.

Pete and Ricky turned at the doorway to see Indy load the last of the equipment on the truck and climb in. As the pickup drove off, Pete noticed Joey and Will standing at the edge of the park, glowering across the street at them. He nudged his brother and Ricky grinned. "Yikes," he said, "are they mad!"

Inside the restaurant the children found a special table set up for them. On it was a club banner and a huge cake with pink frosting and the faces of Punch and Judy in red and white icing.

Pam lifted Sue so that she could see the top of the cake.

The little girl's eyes grew big. "O-oh!" she exclaimed and with that her finger dabbed into the icing.

"No!" cried Pam and Holly together.

"Not now, Sue!" exclaimed Pete.

"Later," said Ricky, rolling his eyes.

After everyone was seated, the children saw their father hurry in and take his place at the speakers' table. As the chairman rapped for order, Mr. Hollister winked at his children. They beamed and Holly wiggled her fingers at him.

After the meeting had started, Mr. Hollister rose to introduce his children and their friends. Then the men sang a welcome song to the youngsters and everyone clapped.

Pete stood up and thanked the Rotary members for their kindness.

When the meal was over, the club president excused the youngsters so that they might carry their pennies to the *Times* office. Once more the sacks were lifted by Dave, Pete, Pam, Ricky and Nada. Ann and Holly followed, each holding one of Sue's hands.

As they walked out of the restaurant, Ricky blinked at the bright sun while the others went ahead and crossed the street on the green light.

Holding the bag of pennies tightly against his chest with both hands, Ricky hurried along just as the light was about to turn red.

He had hardly stepped from the curb when suddenly Joey Brill raced past. The larger boy hit the bag of pennies with his fist, batting it from Ricky's hands.

The sack landed in the street with a *thunk!* and ripped apart, pennies flying in all directions!

CHAPTER 4

A YELLOW NOTE

RICKY stopped short and looked around wildly at the hundreds of pennies rolling this way and that in the intersection. The light, meanwhile, turned and cars started, only to stop with screeching brakes.

Traffic halted in both directions as Ricky and several passersby bent down to pick up the coins. The other Hollisters, Dave, Nada and Ann quickly returned when they heard the tooting horns. A woman gave them an empty shopping bag to put the money in. And Officer Cal, still on patrol, drove up, with his red police car light flashing.

After directing the autos to pass through a small lane where the pennies had been picked up, the policeman asked Ricky what had happened.

"Joey Brill did it!" the boy declared.

All the time, the grinning bully sat watching from a park bench with Will Wilson.

Officer Cal walked over to them and spoke sternly. "Did you knock the pennies from Ricky Hollister's hands?"

"Who, me?" Joey asked.

"Yes, you."

"I ran past him, if that's what you mean," Joey replied glibly.

"Come with me, both of you," Officer Cal ordered. The boys followed him into the street, where the policeman addressed all those who were gathering the pennies.

"Joey and Will are going to pick up the rest of them," he said.

"Gee whiz!" Will began, but the officer's stern look spelled no nonsense.

Dave turned over the shopping bag to Joey. Then the two bullies, grumbling under their breath, started to pick up the coins while Officer Cal detoured the autos around them.

Now the Hollisters and their friends stood at the curbside looking at the hapless pair. Fifteen minutes later Joey stood up straight and said, "Ow! My back! There, you have all your pennies!"

Officer Cal spoke up. "How many should there be, Pete?"

"Fourteen hundred and seventy," was his reply.

"Count 'em," the policeman ordered Joey.

"Gee, I'm not good at arithmetic," the boy protested.

"Count 'em," came Officer Cal's order.

"All right," muttered Joey. He and Will lugged the shopping bag over to the park bench followed by the other children and the policeman.

"One, two, three, four—" Joey began to make piles of one hundred pennies. Twice he miscounted and had to start all over again. Pete and Pam looked

34

on with straight faces. But Holly and Ricky could hardly contain their glee over the bully's punishment.

Finally, the last coin was counted. "There are one thousand, four hundred and sixty-five pennies," said Joey. The corners of his mouth were turned down.

"Then five pennies are missing," Officer Cal said.

"What do you want me to do?" asked the bully.

"Find the other five cents."

"But we've looked and looked."

"Here, I have five pennies in my pocket," Will said. "Take 'em, Joey, or we'll be here the rest of the afternoon."

With all the coins accounted for, the ten pounds of pennies were put back in the shopping bag. Joey and Will stomped off, and as they passed Pete Hollister they whispered dire vows of vengeance.

The blond boy paid no attention to them. He thanked Officer Cal for his help, then led the others down the street to the newspaper office.

As the children marched in the front door carrying the bags of pennies, a photographer awaited them. Flashlights popped as pictures were taken, and the coins deposited on the desk of the editor.

Mr. Speed was there and had the Hollisters give the full story of their puppet show.

"You've done a fine job," the editor told them and wished them luck. "After all," he said, "one good turn deserves another."

Pam shivered at the thought. Maybe—just maybe

—luck would favor her with a prize from the essay contest.

After leaving the newspaper office, the children went straight to their homes. When the Hollisters reached their driveway, they saw their mother and raced across the green lawn to tell her about the penny adventure.

"How wonderful!" Mrs. Hollister declared after hearing all about the Punch and Judy show. "It's so thoughtful to help other people. Now we can help ourselves."

"Help ourselves to what?" Pete asked. "To some more cookies?"

"To the lawn mower," Mrs. Hollister replied. "Everybody has been so busy with puppets and shows that I'm afraid our lawn needs a good manicuring."

"Okay, Mom," Ricky spoke up. "Pete and I'll do it."

"Me too," Holly said. "I'll help weed the flower beds."

"And if you find any worms, can I give them to the robins?" asked little Sue.

In a few minutes the Hollister yard was filled with the sound of a power mower, hedge clippers and grass cutters.

"Mmmm, how good the fresh grass smells," Pam said as she clipped around the petunia bed.

Just then Mrs. Hollister opened the door and called out, "Pam, a telephone call for you."

The blond girl dropped the shears, wiped her hands on the grass and hurried into the house.

"Maybe it's long distance," said her mother. "The voice is very faint."

Pam picked up the phone. "Hello?"

"Pam Hollister?" came a masculine voice.

"Yes, that's right."

"I have good news for you," the caller continued.

Pam tingled from her head to her toes. "Good news? What is it?"

"You have won third prize in the contest."

Pam's jaw fell open. She was too excited to speak.

"Hello? Are you still there?" came the voice.

"Ye—yes," Pam said. "You mean I won the palomino horse?"

"So you did. You will be notified in tomorrow's mail. Good day."

Pam put down the receiver slowly and turned as if in a trance. Then suddenly she sprang into action. "Mother, I won!" she exclaimed. She put her arms around Mrs. Hollister and danced for joy.

"Goodness, you're getting me out of breath," her mother declared. The other youngsters, having heard the shouts, clomped into the house.

"What's all the excitement?" asked Pete.

When Pam told him she had won a palomino, cheers went up from her brothers and sisters.

"Now Domingo can have a playmate!" exclaimed Sue. She was talking about the Hollisters' burro.

"And we can build another stall in the garage," Ricky declared.

37

"But there won't be enough room for the car," said Holly.

"A horse is more important than a car," Ricky answered with authority.

Pete grinned. "What are you going to name it, Pam?"

"She doesn't even know if it's a boy or a girl," Holly said. "We'll have to wait."

Sue wanted to name the new pet Black Beauty, but Pam told her that palominos were a beautiful gold color.

"Then how about Goldilocks?" Sue asked quickly.

Names for the horse and plans to house the new pet were topics for discussion the rest of the day.

"Oh dear," Pam said at bedtime, "I don't think I'll be able to go to sleep waiting for that letter tomorrow morning." But the day's excitement had been so great that she fell asleep smiling, dreaming of frolicking horses.

Next morning, after breakfast, the five Hollisters stationed themselves along Shoreham Road from the front of their home to Dave Hunter's house, a quarter of a mile away. Pam stood by the postbox and Holly at the end of the line.

"When I first see Mr. Barnes, I'll call out," she had told her older sister.

The morning sun shone down through the leafy branches as the shadows danced along the pavement. Finally Holly cried, "I see Mr. Barnes!" Word was passed down the line to Pam, who waited with heart pounding.

"Oh, Mr. Barnes!" Holly called out. "Do you have a letter for my sister Pam? She lives at one-twenty-four Shoreham Road."

The postman smiled as he approached her. "Number one-twenty-four, you say? Hmmm. Yes, I have a letter for Pam."

Holly turned and dashed along the road, her pigtails flying in the breeze. "Pam got a letter!"

Sue took up the shout, then Ricky. When they reached Pete, the blond boy said, "All right, all right, we got the message."

All four ran to Pam and crowded around her, awaiting the arrival of Mr. Barnes. Pam felt too dignified to race to meet him. But she did walk along the road for a few paces, her face flushed with excitement as she met the postman.

"By jiminy," Mr. Barnes said as he handed Pam her letter, "this must be a very important one."

"Yikes, it is!" Ricky declared.

Pam thanked Mr. Barnes, looked down at the envelope, and the expression on her face suddenly changed. She noted that her name had not been typed. It was written in pencil in block letters. A twinge of fear gripped her as she held the letter tightly in her hand and marched straight into the house.

"What's the matter, Pam?" Ricky asked as he and the others followed their sister into the living room.

Pam sat down on the sofa and opened the envelope. In it was a folded piece of yellow paper. She opened it and drew a long, stifling sigh. On the pa-

39

per was a picture of an old sway-backed, funny-looking horse, and printed beneath it was: *The joke's on you! Joey.*

Pam covered her face with her hands and sobbed bitterly.

"Oh, what a terrible thing to do!" Pete said between clenched teeth.

"Then it was Joey who telephoned last night," Holly said.

Pam nodded her head, still weeping over her disappointment.

When Mrs. Hollister came upstairs from her basement laundry room she put an arm around her heartbroken daughter. "Don't worry, dear," she told Pam. "Nothing good will come to boys who play mean tricks like that."

"Yes," Ricky said, "and we still have Domingo."

Pam daubed at her red eyes, sniffled a bit and managed a weak smile.

"And maybe the palomino wouldn't get along with Domingo," declared Sue seriously.

"Well," Mrs. Hollister said, "all is not lost. We're having a party this afternoon."

"Whose birthday?" Ricky piped up.

"Nobody's," his mother replied. "But since Nada's leaving tomorrow for Italy, Mrs. Hunter and I thought it would be nice to have all the children over to say good-by."

After Pam had washed her face in cool water and brushed her hair, she joined the others in the back yard where they had begun preparing for the party.

Her brothers and sisters were very kind to her, and Holly said, "You just lost a make-believe palomino, but that isn't nearly as bad as losing a real great-uncle the way Nada did."

Pam kissed her sister and they set about to spread the long picnic table in the shade of a tree.

At lunch time Mr. Hollister came home and brought a copy of the morning paper. The children's pictures were in it with the story of their puppet show.

"I hope Joey sees that," said Ricky. "It'll make him feel terrible."

Promptly at three o'clock Nada, Ann and Jeff arrived with their mothers. Mrs. Hunter was carrying a large, covered cake dish. As she put it on the picnic table, chubby Donna Martin ran into the yard, followed shortly afterward by Dave Mead.

"This is a going-away party," Mrs. Hollister told the children. "We hope that Nada will remember her friends in the United States."

"Yes, I will," the dark-haired girl said shyly. "I would like to stay longer, but we must search for Uncle Giovanni."

"Oh, I wish you didn't have to go," Pam said.

"We may all meet again one day," Mrs. Boschi remarked brightly.

"Now how about some games," Mrs. Hollister suggested. "This is no time to be sad."

"Who wants a burro ride?" Pete called out. When cries of "I do!" filled the yard, he went to the garage and paraded Domingo into view. The burro was wearing a bright ruffled collar of crepe paper and a large yellow plume tied to the top of his head.

"Oh!" exclaimed Nada delightedly. "*L'asinello!* A little donkey!"

Holly and Sue proudly announced that they had decorated their pet. The feather had come from an old hat of their mother's which they had found in the attic.

Nada had the first ride. She dimpled and smiled as Pete led Domingo around the yard three times. After the Italian girl slid off the burro's back, the other children took turns riding. Then the boys played leapfrog and were joined by Holly. She jumped very well over Ricky and Jeff. But Pete proved too tall for her, and the tomboy tumbled head over heels onto the grass.

"Let's play musical chairs," Pam said, "so everybody can join in." She, Holly and the boys hustled into the house and returned with enough chairs for the game. Donna helped Sue carry out their small doll piano. Mrs. Hollister put it on top of the picnic table. Then Ricky dashed inside and out again, bringing his small harmonica.

"What are you doing with the mouth organ?" Jeff Hunter asked.

"I'm going to play it."

When the chairs had been put in place, Mrs. Hollister played a tinkling tune on the toy piano. Ricky joined in on his harmonica as he marched round and round with the other children. When the music stopped they scrambled for the chairs. Pete was left standing.

"You're out!" Holly cried impishly.

The music started again. Around they marched. When the tune stopped this time, Ricky kept playing his mouth organ. Holly went on marching. When the rush for seats was over, the pigtailed girl stood alone, looking disappointed.

"No fair! You fooled me, Ricky," she protested.

"I'm sorry," he replied happily. "I didn't hear the piano stop."

But before Holly could answer him, Mrs. Hollister started playing again. This time Ricky did not scoot as fast as Sue and was left out of the game. Finally only Nada and Dave Mead remained.

The tinkling piano sounded merrier than ever, and the two children laughed as they circled the last seat cautiously. The music stopped. Nada slid onto the chair. *And Dave sat on her lap!*

What a howl went up from the children! When Dave realized what had happened, he jumped off so fast that he flopped onto the grass. While they were still laughing, Mrs. Hunter announced it was time for ice cream and cake. Everyone seemed to enjoy the treat except Holly, who cast sidewise glances at her red-haired brother for his harmonica trick.

When the party was over, the Boschis thanked everyone and said good-by.

"We'll see you in the morning before you go," Pam promised.

Dave sat on her lap!

That night Pete threw himself on his bed and exclaimed, "Crickets! What an exciting day!"

"Yes, but I've got to find a way to get that Joey!" Ricky told his brother.

The redhead awakened in the middle of the night, but instead of going back to sleep, he pondered how he could play a trick on the bully.

As Ricky was thinking, he heard a noise from outside. He got up and looked out the window. A car was coming into their driveway with its lights off. In the darkness the auto crept alongside the house. When it stopped, the door opened quietly and the dim figure of a man stepped out. Zip, who was sleeping on the porch, gave a low growl.

Ricky leaped across the room and shook Pete. "Sh-sh, don't make any noise," he said. "Come on downstairs. Somebody's sneaking around our yard!"

Without awakening the others, the boys tiptoed down the steps and across the living room. When they reached the porch the stranger was about to turn the knob on the screen door. Pete quickly switched on the light!

CHAPTER 5

GROWN-UP RICKY

INSTANTLY lights flooded the front porch, showing the man who was trying to enter their house.

It was Uncle Russ!

"Crickets!" Pete exclaimed softly. "Uncle Russ, we didn't expect you."

Russell Hollister was their father's younger brother. He was taller than the children's father, slender, and handsome. With his wife, Aunt Marge, and their two children, Teddy and Jean, he lived in the town of Crestwood. Uncle Russ was a cartoonist whose comic strips appeared in newspapers all over the country.

"Sh-sh!" the visitor said with a big grin as he entered the house. "Don't wake anybody up." Quietly he put down the overnight bag he was carrying.

"Yikes," Ricky said, tugging at his uncle's hand, "why didn't you telephone us you were coming?"

"I made wonderful time on the turnpike," the cartoonist said, "—expected to stop at a motel a hundred miles back, but it was a nice cool evening so I kept on driving."

46

He explained that he had not called for fear of awakening the family.

Zip wagged his tail and licked Russ Hollister's free hand.

"I'll sleep on the couch down here," their uncle said.

"You don't have to do that," Pete replied.

"Of course not," Ricky spoke up manfully. "Uncle Russ, you can sleep in my bed and I'll crawl in with Pete."

"Sure you won't mind?" The boys assured him they would not and Pete picked up his uncle's bag.

The cartoonist slipped off his shoes, and tiptoed upstairs with his nephews.

After tousling Ricky's red hair, Uncle Russ whispered good night. The two boys got into bed together and all was quiet again.

Holly was the first one to open her eyes the next morning. She padded over to where Sue was sleeping and roused her sister. "I want to play a trick on Ricky," she said, "because he fooled me at musical chairs yesterday."

Sue sat up on her elbows, blinked her big eyes and yawned. "What kind of a trick?"

"I could tickle him or something."

"All right, but we must be very quiet," Sue cautioned Holly.

Still in their pajamas, the two sisters, with big smiles on their faces, walked quietly to Ricky's room. In the dim morning light Holly pushed open the door gently. The sleeper in Ricky's bed was curled

47

up with the light blanket pulled over his head. The bottom of the cover had come untucked and lay loosely over his feet.

Holly tiptoed to the dresser and picked up a hairbrush. Sue could hardly keep herself from giggling as she watched her sister carefully lift the blanket, reach under and tickle the toes with the brush bristles.

Suddenly, with a cry of surprise, the sleeping figure bounded awake and stood in the middle of the floor rubbing his eyes, Holly looked up at the man in amazement and Sue dashed out of the room, running for her mother.

"Help, something terrible has happened! Ricky's grown up!" Sue cried out.

The girl's cry alerted the entire house. Taking Sue with them, Mrs. Hollister and Pam hurried into the boys' room to see what had happened. When they saw Russ Hollister, Holly and her brothers shaking with chuckles, they began to laugh, too.

"So, this is Ricky grown up," Mrs. Hollister said, knotting the belt of her dressing gown.

"I thought I was tickling Ricky's toes," Holly admitted sheepishly.

Then questions began to bombard the cartoonist. "What are you doing in Shoreham?"

"Where are Teddy and Jean?"

"Will you stay with us for a visit?"

Their uncle stretched his arms over his head, winked and said, "I'll answer all your questions at

The sleeping figure bounded awake.

breakfast, provided your mother makes flapjacks for me."

"Yikes!" Ricky said. "Can my mother make flapjacks!"

In little more than half an hour everyone had washed and dressed, and the batter was bubbling on the griddle.

"I think it would be fun to eat out of doors," Mrs. Hollister said.

"Oh yes!" Pam exclaimed, and ran to spread the picnic table which they had used for Nada's party the day before. Soon there were stacks of pancakes, crisp bacon, maple syrup and brimming glasses of milk ready for the hungry Hollisters.

"Mmmm, good," Uncle Russ said as the family enjoyed their breakfast. "Now I feel in the mood for talking."

The cartoonist, with Holly on one side and Sue on the other, said that he was on his way to Italy.

"Yikes!" Ricky cried out. "That's great! You can help Nada solve her mystery."

Uncle Russ put down a forkful of pancakes which he was about to eat. "A mystery in Italy?" he said. "Don't you children have enough mysteries to solve in America?"

"Oh, it isn't our mystery," Pam replied. "Ann Hunter's Italian friend lost her great-uncle."

"Hush!" Holly said. "Why don't you let Uncle Russ tell what *he's* doing?"

"Holly, you're on my side," her uncle said, giving Pam a hug with one arm. "I'm going to Milan."

"What for?" Pete asked.

The cartoonist said that Milan was the comic strip center for all Europe. He was going to arrange a contract to have his cartoons published in many foreign countries.

"Gee whiz, Uncle Russ," Holly said, "I didn't know you could speak so many languages."

"I can't," came the reply. "All the translating is done right there in Milan."

"That's 'citing," said Sue as she wiped a drop of syrup from her chin. "Are Teddy and Jean and Aunt Marge going with you?"

Uncle Russ told them that his wife and two children were visiting Aunt Marge's relatives on the West Coast. "So I have to make the trip all by myself. But I have a good idea," he added with a grin, "to keep from getting lonesome." While Mrs. Hollister poured more milk for Sue, he went on: "I'd like to take Pete and Pam as my guests on this trip."

Everyone stopped eating and looked at the cartoonist in amazement. "What's so unusual about that?" their uncle asked playfully. "You have your passports, don't you?"

"Sure we do," Pete said.

"But what about the rest of us?" Holly asked with a disappointed look.

Their uncle replied that he could not take them all. Some other time the younger children might accompany him on one of his jaunts.

"For goodness sakes, Russ," Mr. Hollister exclaimed, "that's very generous of you!"

Pam looked at Ricky, Holly and Sue, then at her mother. "I don't think we should go," she said. "We've always gone everywhere together."

"But crickets, we're pretty big now!" Pete protested. "I'd like to go with you, Uncle Russ."

Holly pursed her lips and twisted her pigtail round and round. "You go, too, Pam," she said.

"Yes, you don't have to watch for the mailman any more now," Ricky added.

The children's mother spoke up and said, "I think that would be a wonderful idea. How long will you be away, Russ?"

"That all depends," came the answer, "on an extra-special thing I have to do."

"Something more besides your cartoons?" Pete asked.

Their uncle nodded.

"Like what?" Ricky said.

"Sue, will you do me a favor?" the cartoonist asked.

The little girl pushed her empty plate from her and said, "Yes, Uncle Russ."

"If you'll run upstairs and get the cardboard box from my suitcase, I'll show you what the extra-special thing is."

The little girl put down her napkin and raced into the house. In the stillness of the morning they could hear her footsteps mounting the stairs to the bedroom.

"It will be quite a surprise to you all, I know," Uncle Russ said as they waited for the errand girl to return.

Suddenly everybody jumped to hear a *bang—bang—bang*. It sounded like someone falling downstairs!

"Oh dear!" Mrs. Hollister exclaimed. "I hope nothing has happened—" They all dashed into the house and looked at the staircase. Sue stood on the top step. The suitcase lay at the bottom.

"Ow!" Uncle Russ said, putting a hand to his forehead and wincing. "If what's in that suitcase is broken, the President won't like me."

"What President?" Pete asked.

"Of the United States of America!"

CHAPTER 6

WHO'S WHO?

"Yikes," Ricky said, "is this some kind of riddle, Uncle Russ?"

Sue's voice came from the top of the stairs. "I didn't mean to be naughty," she said, descending one step at a time, "but I couldn't open your suitcase, Uncle Russ." Her face puckered into a frown. "I tried to carry it down and it slipped."

The cartoonist tugged at the zipper on his bag and it came open. As the Hollister family looked on, intrigued, Uncle Russ carefully lifted out a cardboard box. He removed the lid. Inside was an object wrapped in white tissue paper, which made a crinkling noise as he carefully took it off.

There was a beautiful pink and white seashell, as large as Ricky's head!

The cartoonist turned it over in his hands and breathed a sigh of relief. "It's not broken, thank goodness."

"Then the President won't be angry with you," Holly said.

"Crickets!" Pete exclaimed, scratching his head. "What's it all about, Uncle Russ?"

"It's an unusual story," he replied. The children sat on the stairs and Mr. and Mrs. Hollister listened with great interest as their guest began to talk.

The President of the United States, he said, had found this perfect shell many years before on a South Pacific island. Now he wanted to have a cameo made of it to present to the First Lady on her birthday.

"A cameo! What's that?" asked Ricky.

Mrs. Hollister explained to her children that a cameo is a piece of jewelry made by carving a beautiful shell.

"That's right," the cartoonist added. "This particular shell has a smooth piece of delicate pink. See it here?" he pointed. "A famous Italian artist named Pietro Caramagna is going to cut this part out and carve it into a cameo to resemble the First Lady's face."

"How interesting!" Pam said. "And are you the messenger who's taking the shell to Italy, Uncle Russ?"

He nodded, smiling. "I know Signor Caramagna well," he explained, "and I know the President's secretary, too. He asked me to meet Pietro in Milan and deliver the shell to him."

Pam made a dash to their encyclopedia set and in a short time had learned many things about cameos. She discovered that the art of making them originated in Mesopotamia and Egypt.

"Do they always have ladies' faces on them?" Ricky asked in a bored voice.

"No," replied Pam. "It says that the Greeks and Romans had them carved with battle and hunting scenes as well as portraits. It must be very hard to do," she added, and read that the artisans cut the figures into the top layer of the shell, so that it stands out in relief against a different-colored layer underneath.

"And listen to this," Pam went on. "In the dark ages the art of cameo-making died out. But it was revived in Italy during the Renaissance. Then cameos were made into wrist bands, earrings, necklaces and brooches."

Uncle Russ added, "Italian shell engravers are experts. Signor Caramagna has a factory and employs many artisans."

"How thrilling!" Mrs. Hollister said. "To think that this shell will be made into jewelry for the President's wife in the White House!"

The youngsters looked proudly at their uncle, who knew so many important people.

Mr. Hollister spoke up. "Russ, you'd better be very careful of that shell."

"That's right, John," his brother replied with a grin. "That's why I need two bodyguards to take on my trip to Milan."

"Here's one," Pete said, standing very erect.

"Pam, you be the other," Holly urged, putting her arm around her sister's waist. "We won't mind if you go, honest."

"I think Holly is right," Mrs. Hollister agreed. "If

Uncle Russ is willing to take you, I think that's grand."

Pam beamed. "I'll go with you, Uncle Russ, and I have just the thing in which to carry that shell." She hastened upstairs and returned a few minutes later with a square cosmetic case of her mother's. She fitted the box into it snugly. "I won't let it out of my sight from here to Milan," she said.

"Yikes, Pete and Pam are going to Italy!" Ricky shouted and did two somersaults on the living room carpet.

Pam took her mother aside and asked if she would let her know immediately if she should win a minor award in the essay contest.

"Of course I will, darling," Mrs. Hollister promised. "Now we have lots to do to get ready for your trip."

After helping with the morning chores, Pam hurried to Ann Hunter's house to tell the exciting news. "Oh, Nada, guess what," she said as the Italian girl came to the door to greet her. "We're going to Italy!"

Breathlessly, Pam related Uncle Russ's plans to the two girls. "And while we're there," she promised Nada, "we'll try to solve the mystery of your uncle's disappearance."

"Oh, if only you could!" replied the girl, then added, "You must learn a few words of Italian."

"Good," Pam said. "Let's go to my house and find a nice quiet place, so you can teach Pete and me."

The three girls skipped back to the Hollister home. Pete suggested that they go out in their rowboat on the lake, where no one could disturb them. Quickly Pam collected four pencils and tablets and the children hurried to the dock.

Pete rowed, while Nada sat in the front and Pam and Ann in the rear seat. The water was calm and shimmery in the morning sunlight. As Pete shipped the oars and turned around to face the Italian girl, Ann giggled. "You look like a teacher in front of a class, Nada!"

"And the first word you are going to learn is Hello," the dark-haired visitor replied with a smile.

Pam passed out pencils and paper. In big letters Nada printed c-i-a-o and held it up for her pupils to see.

Pete grinned. "Do you say it or sneeze it?"

"It is pronounced chow," said Nada.

"Chow," they all repeated and copied the letters on their tablets.

"It can also mean good-by," the Italian girl told them.

"A double-duty word!" said Pam.

"Another way to say good-by is *arrivederci*," Nada went on. "That's more formal and means 'until we meet again.'"

"How about please?" Pam asked.

"Please is *per favore* and thank you is *grazie*."

"Per fa-vor′-ay," the pupils chorused. "Grat′-see-ay."

"Pray′-go!" said Nada and printed p-r-e-g-o.

"It is pronounced chow," said Nada.

"That means you're welcome?" guessed Pam.

"Right," replied the teacher. She pointed to herself. "*Mi chiamo* Nada Boschi." Then she nodded to Ann. "Now tell us what you are called."

"*Mi chiamo* Ann Hunter," said her friend and giggled.

"Good," praised Nada. "And if you want to ask a stranger what his name is, you say *come si chiama.*" Her glance rested on Pete.

"*Mi chiamo* Pete Hollister," he replied promptly and they all laughed.

After they had practiced for a while, Mrs. Hollister called them from the dock and Pete rowed to shore.

"Pam," said her mother, "we have some important matters to discuss about your clothes. I'm sure you'll excuse her, won't you, girls?"

"Yes, Mrs. Hollister," Nada said politely.

"*Ciao,*" said Pam with a smile, and her friends answered "*ciao.*"

"That reminds me," spoke up Pete, "I'm hungry."

"Lunch in an hour," said Mrs. Hollister cheerfully.

Promptly at noon she kept her promise with melted cheese sandwiches, milk and fudge cake. The children had just finished eating, when Nada, her mother and the Hunters drove up to the house and stopped. Mrs. Hollister and the children went out to the car to greet them.

"We've come to say *arrivederci,*" Mrs. Boschi

said, smiling. "And we're thrilled to hear that Pete and Pam are coming to Italy."

"I wish we were going, too," Mrs. Hollister replied.

"If the children should come to Rome they must be sure to call us," the Italian woman said.

"I brought you something," Nada told Pam, and reached into her purse. She drew out a tiny puppet head. "Uncle Giovanni made several of these. He always carried one for a good luck charm. It's just like the regular-sized Punch faces that he carves. You can recognize it by this." She pointed to a funny little mole on the side of Punch's big nose.

"May I keep this?" Pam asked.

"It's yours," Nada replied, "and here's something else, too." She handed Pam a small picture of her great-uncle.

"Oh, isn't he handsome," Pam exclaimed, looking at the small photo. Giovanni Boschi was an aristocratic-looking man. He had a straight nose, deep-set dark eyes, bushy white hair and a small white goatee.

"Crickets," Pete said. "We should be able to recognize him anywhere!"

"*Grazie*," Pam said, and bent over to kiss Nada's cheek.

As the car drove off, Pete nudged his sister. "Those are a couple of good clues to start with."

"Oh, I can hardly wait to go!" Pam replied.

The next two days moved by like a dream for

Pete and Pam. They hastily prepared to fly across the Atlantic Ocean with Uncle Russ. Finally, on Monday, came the moment to leave the house. Mrs. Hollister was at the wheel of their station wagon, while her husband drove his brother's car.

"Everyone ready?" the children's mother called out.

The chorus of yeses was interrupted by the ringing of the telephone.

"You get out and see who that is, Ricky, please," Mrs. Hollister said. The boy leaped out of the station wagon and raced into the house.

"Ricky Hollister speaking," he said.

The voice on the other end was deep and clear. "I have a message for Pam Hollister. She has won—"

"You can't fool us, Joey!" Ricky cut in. "Besides, we're in a hurry. Good-by!" He hung up and raced outside.

"Nothing important!" Ricky said as he jumped back into the station wagon. As the two vehicles pulled out of the driveway, Ricky's eyes bugged wide. There were Joey and Will, sitting astride their bikes at the curb near the house.

All the way to the airport Ricky pondered over the strange turn of events. Was it really Joey who had telephoned? How did he get in front of their house so quickly?

"Yikes," he thought. "Who's who, anyhow?" He wondered about it as he watched Pete, Pam and

Uncle Russ check their baggage and start across the runway toward their airplane.

Minutes later the great aircraft was in the sky, and it seemed no time at all before they had changed planes at New York for the transatlantic crossing.

"Pinch me, Pete," Pam said when they were thousands of feet in the air. "Is this really real?"

"Of course it is," Pete said. "That's a real ocean down there. See that tiny little ship?"

Before long a delicious luncheon was served, and when the meal was finished, Pam leaned back. She had started to doze when someone tapped her on the shoulder.

Pam looked up to see a blue sleeve with four gold bars on it.

"Crickets," Pete said, "wake up! It's the captain of the airplane!"

"Are you Pam Hollister?" the officer asked her.

Pam nodded yes in surprise.

"I have an urgent message for you!"

CHAPTER 7

AN UNPLEASANT MIX-UP

PAM Hollister's hand trembled with excitement as she read the note which the airplane captain had given her.

"Oh!" she exclaimed. "Oh no!"

"What happened?" Pete cried in alarm.

Even the usually smiling Uncle Russ looked tense, and Pam said, "I won the first prize in the contest. An around-the-world trip for two! Mother was notified."

The captain smiled. "I knew you would be pleased," he said, and added that if Pam had a return message he would radio it to America.

Several passengers had turned their attention to the trio. When Pete told them about Pam's exciting news they nodded and smiled. One woman, seated across the aisle from Pam, said, "But you're already on a trip. Maybe they'll give you money instead of the tickets."

Pam shook her head. "I wouldn't want that," she said.

The Hollisters discussed the problem as the great

plane whizzed over the ocean. "Maybe Pam ought to go back," Uncle Russ suggested.

"But that seems like a waste of time," she said.

"You're right, of course," her uncle replied.

After sitting in silence for a few minutes, Pam turned to the other two, her face alight with excitement. "I know what we could do!" she exclaimed. "Instead of a trip around the world for two, maybe I could have a trip halfway around the world for four."

"I don't get it," Pete said.

"Don't you see?" Pam went on. "Then Mother, Sue, Holly and Ricky could use the tickets and join us in Italy."

"You certainly are a generous girl," her uncle said with admiration. Smiling he added, "Come to think of it, Pam, it's a great plan. If your mother and the other children come, you could stay in Italy longer than I will."

"Until we solved the mystery of Giovanni Boschi!" Pete declared.

Pam wondered where they could all meet. "First find out if it can be done," Uncle Russ advised. He gave her a pencil and a paper and she composed a message to be radioed back to her folks.

Accompanied by a stewardess, Pete and Pam went forward to deliver the note to the captain. When he had read it, he smiled broadly. "A great idea, and it should be fun," he said, handing the message to his radio operator.

By the time the plane landed in Milan, Russ Hollister was as excited as his niece and nephew. "Your mother has the name of our hotel," he said. "After she makes the inquiry about the prize, she can contact us there."

Pam clutched the cosmetic case tightly as they debarked from the aircraft. In the terminal, Uncle Russ said, "Pete, you and Pam watch for our bags at the unloading platform while I get some American money changed to Italian."

Other passengers milled about the long low platform where the baggage was to be delivered. Pete glanced about, noting that the passageway to the exit led past a customs officer seated in a glass enclosed booth. A uniformed guard stood before the corridor.

"Oh, here comes some luggage now," Pam said.

The two children looked on intently as the bags were slid endwise onto the platform. Pete spied his some distance away and hastened over to claim it. Pam stood alone for a moment, rising on tiptoes to peer over the shoulders of the grownups crowding about.

Suddenly she felt a hand clutch at the cosmetic case. It tugged with such force that the handle was torn from Pam's grip. She whirled about to see a stout woman glaring at her.

"Give me that bag!" the woman cried out. "Some nerve, taking other people's luggage!"

"It's mine!" Pam exclaimed. "Please, give it back to me!"

The woman was in no mood to argue. Clutching

a suitcase in one hand and the shell container in the other, the traveler barged through the crowd straight toward the customs officer. At first Pam looked around wildly for Pete or her uncle. Seeing neither, she pushed through the passengers trying to catch up with the woman. By the time Pam reached the customs gate the woman was already showing her passport. Three other passengers stood between her and the frantic girl.

"Stop! Stop!" Pam cried out. "You have my case by mistake!" She tried to push through the line but the uniformed guard halted her.

"I must get that woman," Pam explained to him. "She has my bag."

The woman put the passport into her purse, turned and glared. "That young lady is mistaken," she said, and hurried on.

Pam's heart sank. Uncle Russ had entrusted her with the President's cameo shell and now she had lost it.

"Please, *per favore!* Let me through!" Pam pleaded, annoyed at the guard. "I'll come back right away, just as soon as I get my cosmetic case!"

The woman, meanwhile, was nearly out of sight as she hastened across the airport building toward the taxi stand.

Now the guard did seem confused. "Where's your mother?" he asked her.

"In America—but I can't wait to answer questions," Pam said. "Please let me go. I promise to come back."

The guard waved toward another uniformed officer standing near the baggage counter. The second man hastened over and the two spoke rapidly in Italian.

"Come with me," the second guard said. He escorted her past the customs officer. Once on the other side of the gate, Pam dashed toward the taxi stand. Bursting through the doors, she saw the woman about to enter a cab. The girl raced forward and grasped her cosmetic case with both hands. The stout traveler turned on her in surprise. "Get away from here!" she said.

By this time the guard had caught up with Pam. He spoke English well and asked what was going on.

"This girl is trying to steal my case," the woman said testily.

"You may have one just like it, but this is mine," Pam protested. "Look, my mother's name is on it right here."

All three looked at the plastic identification tag attached to the handle.

"Are you Mrs. John Hollister?" the guard asked the stout woman.

"Why—why no," she said.

"My name is Pam Hollister!" Pam declared.

"Then this case belongs to the girl," the guard said.

The woman looked flustered. "Well, mistakes will happen," she remarked. "My bag looks exactly like that. No, I think it's a little larger."

"This girl is trying to steal my case!"

Pam thanked the guard, turned and hurried back to where she had left her brother. When she arrived at the baggage platform, Pete and Uncle Russ were looking for her.

"Oh, there you are!" her uncle called out. "Pam, where have you been?"

As the girl told her story, Pete spied one remaining piece of luggage on the platform. It was a case, a little larger than the one Pam carried. The stout woman hastened over to it, picked it up and with a haughty turn of her head waddled off.

"Well," Pete said, "at least the cameo shell is safe!"

Russ Hollister praised Pam for her presence of mind as the three collected their own baggage. After showing their passports, they got into a taxi.

"So this is Italy!" Pete said as the cab drove across a level plain toward the city. To the north, in the distance, the travelers could see the dim outline of mountains.

"That's where the Alps begin," Uncle Russ told them. He added that Milan lay in a vast, fertile plain which covered the northern part of Italy.

The cab sped along the highway, entered the busy city and wound its way through streets leading to the heart of Milan. There it pulled up in front of a hotel.

Each of the guests was assigned to separate single rooms. As Uncle Russ entered his, he said, "We'll meet in the lobby in one hour. Signor Caramagna should be there by that time."

Pam handed her uncle the small traveling case. Then she and Pete went into their rooms to refresh themselves after the transatlantic flight.

An hour later the two youngsters met in the lobby, where they found their uncle already chatting with a distinguished-looking Italian gentleman. Mr. Caramagna was tall and had a thin, thoughtful face. His hands were long and slender, but his grip was firm as he shook hands with the Americans.

"Thank you for rescuing the shell," Mr. Caramagna said to Pam, and bowed slightly.

"I am sorry not to have supper with you," the Italian artist went on, "but I must hurry back to Naples with the shell."

"Is that where your factory is?" Pete asked.

"It's between Naples and Pompeii," the man replied, and explained that he would have to work night and day to complete the cameo for the First Lady's birthday.

"We're sorry you can't stay," Uncle Russ said.

Signor Caramagna gestured with his hand. "There is so much work, not only for me but also for everyone in my factory." He told the Hollisters that there was a great demand both for new and antique cameos. "When you come south," he said, "I will show you the greatest collection in Italy on display at the Caramagna cameo factory showrooms."

After transferring the shell into his suitcase, Signor Caramagna bade the Hollisters good-by and left the hotel.

71

"What now?" Pete asked his uncle.

"The Galleria is near here," the cartoonist replied. "Perhaps we could have supper there."

"Crickets! Lead the way," Pete said gaily.

They left the hotel and in a short time came to the most unusual building that either Pete or Pam had ever seen. Straight through the middle of it, like a huge street, was an arcade several stories high. It was covered by a curved glass roof. On both sides of the Galleria were shops and restaurants.

Uncle Russ led them to a café which had tables and chairs out in the open along one side of the arcade. There they had supper and watched the people wandering in and out.

When they had finished, Uncle Russ said, "And now I have a big surprise for you."

"What?" Pam asked.

"You'll see." They walked out through the other end of the Galleria and came upon a breath-taking scene. Before them lay a huge plaza or *piazza*, and on one side loomed a beautiful cathedral.

"Oh!" Pam said. "It's gorgeous!"

"That's called the Duomo of Milan," Uncle Russ said, "and it took four hundred years to build."

"The spires look so lacy," Pam remarked as they walked closer to the ancient church. The travelers admired the scores of statues which decorated the top, one on the tip of almost every spire.

After wandering through the cathedral and back to their hotel, Pete suggested that they visit the police station to inquire about the details of Giovanni

Boschi's disappearance. A cab took them quickly to headquarters, where they found a stern-faced man sitting behind the desk. On it was a sign, *Il Capitano*. He listened to their request.

"It is a mystery to us," the captain said. "We would welcome assistance from anyone." He explained that it had been raining hard on the day when Giovanni Boschi's motorcycle had been found by the side of the road. "It looked as if it had been run over by a car," the captain told them.

"May we visit the place?" Pam asked.

"An unusual request," the officer said. For a few moments he studied the serious faces of his visitors. Then he smiled. "I will arrange it tomorrow. One of my *carabinieri* will meet you in front of the hotel at ten o'clock."

"*Grazie, Capitano*," Pete said, and the officer replied, "*Prego*."

Early next morning, Uncle Russ ordered a rented car and it was brought to the hotel at nine o'clock. Promptly at ten, an Italian police officer appeared on his motorcycle.

"If you will follow me," the carabiniere said, "I shall take you to the scene of the accident."

The motorcycle roared ahead of them, up one street and down another, finally leading the way out of town, east over the Autostrada. Several miles past city limits their escort pulled to the side of the highway and Uncle Russ drove up behind him.

"Here is the place," the policeman told them. The spot he pointed out beside the road was composed of hard-baked mud and a few blades of grass.

As the Hollisters got out of their car, the carabiniere said, "I must leave you now," saluted, and rode off on his cycle.

"We have to look for some clues," Pam said. "Come on, Uncle Russ, you can help us too."

"But where do I begin?" the cartoonist asked. "I'm not a detective like you."

Pam reasoned that if Giovanni Boschi had dropped anything in the mud that day, the chances were it had hardened in the brown earth by this time. She and Pete found sticks and began to scratch the barren earth.

Time after time they dug up bits of stone, but nothing more. Uncle Russ joined them, using a tire iron which he found in the car.

"Nothing around here," Pete said after they had scratched about for nearly an hour. Then he added, "Oh-oh, what's this? A piece of cloth."

Pam leaped to his side and both children dug around it carefully. Then Pete tugged at the cloth and pulled out a small puppet.

"It looks just like the one Nada gave us," Pam declared.

Pete shook the hard mud off the little Punch and Pam wiped him with her handkerchief. On the side of his nose was a mole, Giovanni Boschi's mark.

Pete turned the puppet upside down to look inside the head. But the neck opening, too, was caked with mud. Pete scraped it out, and his fingers touched a piece of paper. Carefully he pulled it free and smoothed it.

Scrawled in pencil was the word *aiuto*.

"This is a marvelous clue!" Pam exclaimed excitedly, "but I wonder what it means!"

The three got back in the car and drove as quickly as they could to the hotel. While their uncle parked, Pete and Pam hastened inside to the concierge at the desk.

"What does this mean?" Pam asked the manager, showing him the note.

The clerk looked at it and then at the children, surprised.

"It says 'help!'" he told them.

CHAPTER 8

A MESSAGE FROM VENICE

"Grazie," Pam said, and wheeled about, nearly bumping into Uncle Russ as he entered the lobby.

"That Italian word meant 'help,'" Pete blurted to his uncle. "I think we should tell the police right away."

With Pam carrying the puppet head and the note, the three drove to the police station and turned over the evidence which they had dug up beside the Autostrada.

The *capitano* was amazed at their discovery. He said it was a definite clue that Giovanni Boschi had been seized by kidnapers.

But who could they be? The police already had contacted many of Giovanni's friends, only to learn that he had no known enemies.

The Hollisters and the officer pondered why anyone would want to kidnap such a nice old man. "Certainly not to force him to make puppets," the policeman said, shaking his head.

"His motorcycle might have been damaged *after* he was caught," Pam reasoned, "to make everyone think he had been in an accident."

The captain nodded. "We thought he might have been injured in the head, lost his memory and wandered away from the scene of the crash. Now we feel positive he was kidnaped," he added.

Pam said that Nada should know about the new clue immediately. The police captain put a call through to Rome. Then he handed the receiver to the American girl.

"Hello, Nada? This is Pam Hollister. Pete and I are in Milan with Uncle Russ." Quickly she told of their discovery.

Watching his sister's face, Pete could see that she was receiving some important news, too. After speaking a few more minutes, Pam hung up and turned to the others.

"Nada and her mother got a postcard from Venice!"

"Sent by Giovanni?" Pete asked.

"They think so," Pam replied. "No words were written on it. Only a sketch of Punch's profile."

"You mean just his big nose and chin?" Pete asked. Pam nodded.

Uncle Russ spoke up. "Sometimes artists can sketch faster than they can write."

Pam told them that the picture postcard showed the Campanile, or tall tower, built alongside St. Mark's Cathedral.

All the while the police captain made notes of what Pam reported. Then he said, "The sketch on the postcard could be a secret message."

Pete and Pam thought so, too. Punch was always

getting into trouble. Maybe Giovanni was saying that he was in trouble also.

The police officer said that he would notify authorities in Venice immediately.

"Let's go there right away, Uncle Russ," Pete said eagerly. "Maybe we can pick up Giovanni Boschi's trail."

The cartoonist shook his head. "I'm sorry, but I can't take you," he said. As the children looked disappointed, he explained that he had a date with a publisher the next morning. He could not postpone it.

On their way back to the hotel, Uncle Russ remarked, "You'll have to be alone most of tomorrow, but I think you can take care of yourselves."

For the rest of the day, the cartoonist took his niece and nephew sight-seeing. They were especially thrilled to see Leonardo da Vinci's original painting of *The Last Supper*. It covered one wall of an ancient building which used to be a dining room for monks.

"How it survived the last war," Uncle Russ said, "is a miracle. This building was a wreck!"

"But it was saved, and restored," Pam observed as she gazed long at the famous painting. As they left the cool church building and stepped once more into the hot Italian sunshine, Pam's thoughts turned again to the missing Giovanni. Although she had enjoyed the tour of Milan, she was impatient to get to work on their latest mystery.

Next morning at breakfast Uncle Russ said, "I

feel bad about not being able to take you to Venice. But while I'm gone today I have something for Pam to do." He reached down to open the briefcase which lay beside his chair. From it he pulled a sketch pad and pencil.

"I'd like you to make some sketches of the Duomo for me," he said. "You and Pete can go onto the roof. The view is magnificent."

He warned the youngsters, however, not to wander farther than the Galleria and the cathedral. "You can come back to the hotel for lunch," he said, then added with a wink, "but don't get lost."

"Don't worry about us," Pete said with a big grin. "We're not like Ricky or Holly."

Uncle Russ clicked his briefcase shut, rose, and left for his day's business.

Pete and Pam wandered out of the hotel and found their way to the Galleria. After exploring some of the shops, they sat at one of the little tables and ordered hot chocolate.

Between sips, Pam sketched the tall, vaulted ceiling as Pete looked on. "Crickets, that's pretty good," the boy said. Even the waiter, in his black jacket, stopped now and then to look at Pam's work. Finally he tapped her on the shoulder and said, "I have a message for you."

"For me?" Pam asked in surprise.

She put down her pencil and reached for a white envelope which the waiter gave her.

"Where'd you get that?" Pete asked.

"A man was sitting here behind you," the waiter

79

told them. "I thought he was admiring your sketch."

Pete turned around in his chair but no man was there now.

"He just left," the waiter said.

Pete grinned. "Maybe the note is complimenting you on your drawing, Pam."

The girl opened the envelope and pulled out a piece of folded white paper. On it were several words in Italian. "What do they say?" she asked, looking up at the waiter.

A frown creased his forehead. "I do not like to tell you," he said, hesitating.

"Crickets!" Pete exploded. "Is it something bad?"

"I'm afraid so," came the reply.

The man shook his head and pursed his lips. "'Give up the search,'" he read. "'You are in danger.'"

Pete looked about the Galleria in dismay. Pam, too, was frightened. She and her brother exchanged a questioning glance. *Who besides the police could know they were seeking Giovanni?*

Pete looked serious and said to the waiter, "Can you describe the man who gave you this note?"

"He was short and had a mustache."

"Thanks," the boy said and paid for their chocolate. In a low voice he added, "Come on, Pam, let's get out of here."

The pair made their way back to the hotel as quickly as possible. "I feel as if we're being followed," Pam remarked as they hastened into the lobby. Pete rang for the elevator, and both went to Pam's room.

"I'm worried," the girl said as she sank into an easy chair.

"It is creepy," her brother agreed. "Somebody must have overheard our conversation with Nada."

"At the police station?"

Pete shrugged. "This is getting to be a real deep mystery."

"I sort of wish we weren't alone," Pam said. "If Ricky and Holly were here they'd say something funny."

Pete and Pam stayed in Pam's room writing postcards to friends in Shoreham until lunch time. Then they went down and ate in the hotel restaurant. Throughout the meal they kept watch for a small man with a black mustache. They saw no one answering the description.

After finishing a dessert of fresh fruit, Pete said, "We just can't sit around the hotel all day, Pam. I think we'll be safe if we take a taxi to the Duomo. Probably no one will look for us on the roof."

The concierge called a cab and in a few minutes the children were standing inside the cool cathedral. They walked past the gigantic pillars to the great altar, then turned left as a sign directed them to the elevator.

They rode up in the small car with several other sight-seers and stepped out onto the marble slabs which covered the ancient Duomo.

"Pete, isn't it glorious!" Pam exclaimed in delight as she looked up at the lofty spires, each with its own intricate carving.

"Crickets!" her brother declared. "It must have taken many lifetimes to do all this work!" They walked to a stone ledge at the edge of the roof and looked down on the city below. Then they strolled around, mingling with other tourists who were taking pictures.

"Look," Pete said, pointing upward to a winding stairway. "You can climb even higher."

Pam replied that she would stay where she was and make a drawing. She found a nook in the shadow of a parapet and sat down on a low stone block.

As Pam put the sketch pad on her lap, she noticed a small, dark man with a thin mustache taking pictures. She nudged her brother. "Look there, Pete."

The boy glanced at the man. He wore a well-tailored suit with a silk tie. His curly hair was brushed back neatly. "There must be thousands of short men with black mustaches in Italy," Pete reminded his sister with a smile.

The man paid no attention to them. He put the camera he had been using on the ledge. Then he unslung a second one from his shoulder and peered through the range-finder.

"He must be a tourist too," Pete observed. As he spoke, a small child brushed past the man's other

Pete leaped forward.

camera and it teetered on the ledge. Pete leaped forward, and grasped it just as it was about to fall.

When the man saw what had happened he smiled. "*Grazie*," he said, and Pete replied, "*Prego*." Then the photographer said something more in Italian.

"I'm an American," Pete told him.

"Ah yes?" the man replied. "But you speak Italian very well."

"We know about a dozen words," the boy replied.

He introduced himself and Pam.

"My name is Gallino. Count Gallino, from Venice." Pam enjoyed the Italian's delightful accent, but still she hung back, a little afraid to engage the stranger in conversation. Pete, however, was less cautious. Soon he was talking to the man about their trip to Italy.

Pam caught her brother's eye and shook her head slightly to warn him. Pete ignored the signal.

"I like Americans," the fellow was saying with a smile, "because they are my best customers." He told them that his family owned a famous glass factory in Venice. Then he put in quickly, "I'd like to get a few more pictures," and he and Pete moved off a distance, still talking.

Now Pam gazed up at the lacy spires which stood out clear against the blue sunlit sky. Her pencil moved rapidly as she sketched the scene before her. So engrossed was she that she did not think about her brother. Finally, her drawing completed, Pam looked around for him. Her heart skipped a beat as her eyes scanned the roof without sight of Pete.

Pam put her sketch on the ledge, stood up and looked about in all directions. Pete and the man had vanished!

CHAPTER 9

A MILLION PIGEONS

TERRIBLE thoughts raced through Pam's mind.
Had her brother been kidnaped by the mustached
man? Where had he been taken? To the same hiding place where Giovanni Boschi was being held?

The girl looked about wildly, and even stood on
the stone block to gaze at the sight-seers milling
about the roof of the Duomo. In the distance she
spied a uniformed attendant showing visitors the
way to the down elevator.

Pam picked up her sketch and pencils and hastened toward the man. In her rush over the shiny,
polished marble slabs a sudden thought struck her.
Pam turned to look up at the main spire which rose
high above the vaulted roof.

She saw two figures leaning over the rail, both
taking pictures. Could they be Pete and the man?
Then a shout reached her ears. "Don't go, Pam! I'll
be right down!"

Pam sighed with relief, and a little shudder shook
her shoulders.

In a few minutes Pete had descended the spiral
stairway from the pinnacle above. He ran up to his

sister with a big smile. "Crickets! You're pale, Pam. Are you all right?"

The girl nodded. "I was a little worried about you," she said.

Count Gallino caught up to Pete and, having overheard what Pam said, declared, "Don't worry, Pam, your brother is safe with me."

At that moment a padre crossed in front of them, leading a group of school children. "*Ciao*," he called out to Count Gallino, who nodded and returned the greeting.

"The Count is on our side," Pete said as the color returned to Pam's cheeks. "He's interested in the Boschi case."

The Italian smiled at Pam. "Your brother told me you had a special mission to accomplish, but he would not say what it was until I had proved my identity. You are cautious," he added, "so I know you are good detectives."

The three chatted a while longer, and Count Gallino said that if they should come to Venice, they must be sure to get in touch with him at the glass factory. "I will be happy to help you," he said with a bow. He shook hands with both children, who then descended in the elevator and walked quickly to their hotel.

"Phew!" Pam said as they entered the lobby. "If I have any more surprises today—" As she spoke, she passed a clump of bushy potted palms.

"Boo!" cried a voice and a little dark-haired figure jumped out at her. Pam gave a small cry, then threw her arms around Sue Hollister. "Honey! Where did you come from!"

"Out of the nowhere into the here," declared Sue, dimpling and repeating a little saying her mother had taught her.

There was a burst of excited laughter from behind the palms and out stepped Holly, Ricky and Mrs. Hollister. People passing through the lobby looked on delightedly as the family embraced.

All the children talked at once until Pete called for quiet. "Let Mother tell it," he said. They sat down on a long sofa in the lobby and Mrs. Hollister told Pete and Pam what had happened. The contest officials had allowed the halfway-around-the-world trip for four. "We can tour Italy together," their mother said, beaming.

Before they had a chance to return to their rooms, Uncle Russ walked in. "Well, I'll be a monkey's uncle!" he exclaimed as Holly and Sue rushed into his arms. There was another outburst of explanations, then he said, "It's lucky that you came now. I have to go immediately to Frankfort, Germany, so I must leave you."

The youngsters were sorry to hear this, but now they had their mother to travel with!

"We must go to Venice as soon as possible," Pete said. "I think Giovanni Boschi is being held a prisoner there."

The rest of the afternoon the family had a jolly time, with Pete and Pam bringing them up to date on the mystery in Italy. After supper Uncle Russ excused himself to write business letters. The others gathered in Mrs. Hollister's room and spread out a big map of Italy on the double bed. Sue perched on a pillow, while Holly and Ricky took off their shoes and climbed up on the counterpane to see better.

"Watch out, Ricky," said Pete, "you're kneeling on Venice."

"Where?" asked his brother, moving aside.

"There," Pam pointed. "It's that spot off the coast."

"The city was built on small islands centuries ago," Mrs. Hollister explained.

"Because the people liked to swim?" Holly asked.

"No," Pete told her. "They thought they'd be safe there from invaders who used to come down over the Alps and make war on towns in Italy." He also told them that the city was laced with canals, which served as the main streets. Dozens of little bridges spanned the waterways.

"What do they do with their automobiles?" asked Ricky amazed.

"Boats are the only means of transportation other than walking," Mrs. Hollister informed him.

Pam, consulting her guidebook, read that water buses were called *vaporetti*. "They stop at various places just as our buses do on the city streets," she read.

"And don't forget the gondolas," Pete reminded her.

"Here's a picture of one," said Pam and held up the guidebook showing a photograph of a long low boat. On the high rear deck stood a man, plying the big oar with both hands.

"That's the gondolier," said Pete.

"Yikes," said Ricky, "that's keen!" Quick as a wink he climbed onto the footboard of the bed and stood up unsteadily. "Look at me," he cried, swinging an imaginary oar. "I'm a chandelier!"

"Gondolier, silly!" Holly said, then shrieked. "Ricky!"

"Watch out!" chorused the others as the boy waved his arms wildly and fell onto the bed right in the middle of the map.

At that moment, there came a knock on the door. Mrs. Hollister opened it to admit Uncle Russ.

"What's going on here?" he asked. "I heard you from the hall."

"We were just studying the map," Ricky said, scrambling off the bed while the others giggled.

Before everyone turned in, Mrs. Hollister decided she would drive the rented car to Venice the next day. She telephoned a hotel there for reservations. Uncle Russ did not know how long he would be in Frankfort, but promised to contact his relatives when he returned to Pompeii for the carved cameo.

"Leave a note with Mr. Caramagna telling me where you are," the cartoonist declared.

The entire family rose early next morning and packed before breakfast. When they had eaten, they went out to the car. In it was a carton of sandwiches and soda which Mrs. Hollister had ordered for their lunch.

Uncle Russ said good-by, and the youngsters set off for Venice with their mother at the wheel. She picked her way through the heavy traffic of Milan, found the Autostrada and headed east. On the way, Pete and Pam pointed out the spot where they had found the puppet head.

After a while the highway passed through countryside covered by wheat fields and vineyards. Every few miles an ancient castle could be seen on top of a small hill, surrounded by a little village.

"I didn't know there were so many castles in Italy," Pam said as the fairy-tale scene unfolded before their eyes.

Mrs. Hollister drove at a careful speed, while other autos whizzed past them on the superhighway. About thirty miles from their destination, the family rested by the roadside and ate their lunch.

"Next stop's Venice!" Ricky called out as the car set off once more.

Half an hour later they drove over a long causeway and Holly cried out, "We're there!"

"Yikes!" Ricky exclaimed. "What'll we do with the car?"

Their mother chuckled. "While you were sleeping last night," she said, "I read all about how to get into Venice."

"Hurray for Mother," Sue chirped. "She's smart!"

Mrs. Hollister proved in a few minutes that she knew exactly what to do. After crossing the causeway, the children saw cars lined up before them at the entrance to a huge parking garage. A polite policeman waved them into the building. Mrs. Hollister drove along a lane on the ground floor and stopped to let everyone out except Pete.

When the baggage had been unloaded she said, "Wait here until Pete and I get back."

Then she drove onto a spiral ramp which led higher and higher. On the fifth floor, Mrs. Hollister parked the car. Then she and Pete walked over to an elevator and descended to the first floor. There they met the others standing beside the baggage, talking to a stout porter in a blue denim shirt.

"We're going to the *vaporetto*," Mrs. Hollister said, and gave the man a handful of coins.

"*Grazie*," he replied, and piled the luggage onto a hand truck. The family followed him out of the building, then across the street to a long wooden wharf. There Mrs. Hollister purchased "bus" tickets at a window and called out, "Stay together now, and follow me."

Still trailing the porter, they moved to the edge of the dock. A vaporetto chugged up alongside. On the deck, front and back, were benches for passengers. In the center of the boat, beneath an elevated structure where the pilot sat, was room for standees and baggage.

Two attendants snubbed the craft tightly to the wharf with stout rope, and passengers piled off in a great hurry.

The wave of people pushed Holly back and broke her grasp from Pam's hand.

"Come on, Holly," the older girl called over her shoulder. The porter hopped on the vaporetto ahead of the family, deposited the baggage and stepped onto the dock again as new passengers swarmed aboard. No sooner had the last one leaped onto the boat when the lines were cast off and the motor started with a roar.

Suddenly Pam cried out, "Holly! Where are you?"

Mrs. Hollister glanced about quickly to count her children. Holly was missing!

"There she is!" Pete sang out. His sister stood on the pier, waving her arms as tears coursed down her cheeks.

"We can't lose Holly!" Ricky cried out. "What are we going to do?"

Just then a gondola swung alongside the vaporetto. Pete leaped onto the deck, much to the surprise of the gondolier, and shouted back to his mother, "Have the pilot stop the boat. I'll get Holly!"

By gesturing, he made the oarsman understand that he wanted to return for his sister.

The man nodded. With strong strokes he guided his craft alongside the dock and Holly hopped into it. The vaporetto, meanwhile, had stopped in the middle of the Grand Canal. The gondola caught up with it in two minutes, and as Pete and his sister jumped aboard, Mrs. Hollister tossed the gondolier a coin. He smiled, waved to the children and pulled away over the choppy water.

Pete leaped into the gondola.

"A fine introduction to Venice!" Mrs. Hollister said with a sigh, as Holly flung her arms around her mother.

Their fright was quickly forgotten as the water bus chugged along the great canal. Boats plied back and forth as the youngsters gazed out at the houses built on the very edge of the canal. Some were three or four stories high with ornate façades and balconies.

"Oh, this is even more beautiful than I thought it would be!" Pam said aloud.

The vaporetto made stops, just like the buses in Shoreham. First it went to one side of the canal, then to the other, and people hopped off and on with great alacrity.

"Crickets! You have to be on your toes," Pete said, "else you get left behind."

After half an hour, the boat came in sight of a beautiful rectangular marble building. "That's the Doges' Palace," Mrs. Hollister said. "Our hotel is quite near it."

The Doges, their mother explained, were the early rulers of Venice. Now the vaporetto came close to the shore and the children could see a great plaza in which stood St. Mark's Cathedral. Beside it was a tall campanile.

"There's the bell tower!" exclaimed Pam. "The one on the postcard from Giovanni!"

"That square is the Piazza San Marco," Mrs. Hollister said.

The plaza vanished as the boat glided past it to

the vaporetto stop. There the Hollisters got off, lugging their baggage onto the dock. Again they were met by a porter, who carried the bags to a hotel on the waterfront nearby.

By the time the family had settled down in their suite, it was the supper hour. When the meal was over, they strolled along the canal, turned the corner at the Doges' Palace, and walked into the Piazza San Marco. Outdoor dining places lined the great square. All was serene as open-air orchestras filled the evening with soft music.

While it grew dark, the travelers ambled through tiny alleys, lined on both sides with shops and restaurants. The maze of byways was crisscrossed with bridges over the smaller side canals.

"This would be a great place to hide someone," Pete told Pam.

She agreed. "I think we're going to have a job finding Giovanni Boschi."

"What do we look for first?" asked Ricky after lingering by the window of a curio shop.

Pam thought it would be best to start at the Campanile. Perhaps the postcard was a clue, the girl thought.

"Good," her mother said, "We'll start first thing in the morning."

As the result of no vehicles on wheels, the city was quiet and restful. That night the children fell off to sleep quickly and before they knew it morning had come.

Breakfast over, the family trooped out into the

96

bright sunshine and headed directly for the Campanile. There Mrs. Hollister purchased tickets to the observation tower and they all stepped into the elevator.

What a view from the top! The children crowded along the railing, looking out over the vast city which lay beneath them. Strollers in the Piazza San Marco looked like tiny puppets moved by invisible strings. And the houses with their terra-cotta roofs looked like a toy village.

The young detectives scanned the city carefully from the four sides of the tower.

"Can you see any clues?" Ricky asked his brother.

Pete had to admit that nothing he saw from the top of the Campanile had given him any idea as to the whereabouts of Giovanni Boschi.

"I've seen enough," Holly said. "Let's go downstairs."

The elevator took them to the bottom of the Campanile. As they walked out onto the piazza, Sue pointed a chubby finger and cried out, "I see him! There he is!"

The children turned and saw a tall elderly man walking across the piazza. Pam gasped. He looked for all the world like Giovanni Boschi! Pete and Pam hastened forward with long steps. They did not want to frighten the man by running.

Then, as they were halfway across the square, the great bells of the church tolled nine. Instantly, from everywhere, swarmed hundreds of pigeons.

"Yikes!" Ricky cried. "There's a million of 'em!"

The birds swooped down toward the far end of the piazza in a black cloud, hiding the white-haired man.

CHAPTER 10

THE SLIPPERY THIEF

THE children stopped short at the sight before them. It seemed that every pigeon in Venice was swooping into the Piazza San Marco. The air was filled with the sound of fluttering wings. The birds finally descended onto the pavement and surrounded two men as they strewed handfuls of corn to feed them.

An American passerby, noting the Hollisters' surprise, said, "The pigeons are fed at nine o'clock every morning. When the bells ring, they know what time it is!"

"Good luck for the pigeons, but bad luck for us," Pete remarked and dashed on ahead in search of the white-haired man. He spied him walking through an archway at the far end of the piazza.

"Mr. Boschi!" Pete called, running up to the elderly gentleman.

The man turned about and observed the boy with sharp blue eyes.

"You are Mr. Boschi, aren't you?"

The man hunched his shoulders and gestured with his hands. "No speak English," he said.

By now the others had caught up with Pete. "We'll have to try our Italian," Pam said.

"*Come si chiama?*" Pete asked the man.

"Rocco Martinelli," the Italian replied, looking politely puzzled.

"Yikes!" Ricky said. "He's not the one after all!"

Pam pulled the picture of Giovanni Boschi from her pocketbook and showed it to the stranger. He raised his eyebrows in surprise and looked at the photograph thoughtfully for a few moments. Then he shook his head, pulled a small card from his pocket and presented it to Mrs. Hollister.

She read it and told the children that the man operated a restaurant in Venice.

Disappointed, the children thanked him. He gave a little bow and everyone said, "*Arrivederci!*"

As the man walked away, Pam opened her purse to put the photograph back, and noticed that the catch on the bag was loose.

"Here, Pete," she said, "you'd better carry this picture and the Punch head Nada gave us. They might fall out of my purse." He tucked them away safely in his pocket as the family started across the piazza toward the Doges' Palace.

The Hollisters entered the ancient building through a wide courtyard, then climbed the stairs to a gallery filled with the largest paintings they had ever seen.

"How beautiful!" Pam breathed with a sigh. "It must have been wonderful living in those ancient days."

Mrs. Hollister reminded her that there were many cruel customs in olden times. "Think of the prisoners who were thrown into the dungeons," she said.

"Crickets, can we see the dungeons?" Pete asked.

Their mother consulted her guidebook and led the children downstairs again. There they crossed a covered bridge over a narrow canal. "This is the Bridge of Sighs," Mrs. Hollister told them. As they glanced down at the water below them she explained that some prisoners who crossed this bridge never saw the outside world again.

"That's creepy!" Holly declared, holding tightly to her mother's hand.

Now the way led down a gloomy stone passageway into the damp interior of the dungeon. Their footsteps sounded muffled as they passed cell after cell with doors of iron bars.

"Only a cat could escape from this place," Ricky observed, as he ran his hand along the cool metal.

After a double right-hand turn, the travelers came to the exit and Pam held the door open for her mother. As she did, a wailing sound came from behind them in the dungeon.

"Yikes!" Ricky said. "What was that?"

"Gracious!" his mother exclaimed. "That sounds like Sue. Where is she?"

"She's not here, that's for sure," said Pete.

As they ran back through the passageway they could hear excited voices and soon came upon a group of sight-seers gathered in front of a cell. There was Sue inside!

"Honey!" Pam cried out. "How did you get in there?"

Not knowing whether to laugh or cry, the frightened child said, "If a cat could get in here, so could I."

"Well then, come out," her mother coaxed her.

"But I can't!"

"Try again."

The little girl stood sideways and put one leg through the bars. Then she squeezed her shoulders through. "Oh dear, Mommy, my head wasn't too big a while ago!" She whimpered.

"Easy now," Pete cautioned. "Don't go too fast."

As the onlookers watched breathlessly, Sue squeezed her head between the iron bars. For a few seconds her nose was flattened, but she slipped through without harm.

"There, come now," her mother said. "If you had eaten a bigger breakfast, Sue, you might never have gotten out."

With the little girl's hand firmly in her own, Mrs. Hollister led her family out into the sunshine. They all took a deep breath of fresh air, which blew in from the Adriatic Sea.

Holly eyed an outdoor café at the edge of the square. "I'm hungry," she said.

"It's too early for lunch," her mother replied. "But we'll go over there and have a snack."

While they were drinking hot chocolate, Mrs. Hollister told them that Venice was famous for its

"How did you get in there?"

glass. "I'd like to send some home to Aunt Marge," she said.

"How about going to Count Gallino's factory?" Pete suggested.

Pam volunteered to phone the Italian and learn exactly how to get to his place. While Mrs. Hollister paid the bill and the others watched people strolling about the piazza, Pam went inside the restaurant and made her phone call. A few minutes later she returned smiling.

"Guess what?" she said. "Count Gallino is sending his special launch to pick us up at our hotel." Pam explained that the factory was located on an island far out in the harbor.

"Yikes! That's keen!" Ricky declared.

Only fifteen minutes later, a sleek powerboat pulled up to the hotel dock where they waited. It had a small cabin and seats for ten people. Count Gallino himself was at the wheel. When he saw the Hollisters he waved. *"Buon giorno,"* he called. "Good day! Welcome to Venice!"

Pete and Pam introduced the rest of their family as each one stepped down into the purring motorboat. Then the Count opened the throttle and they sped across the water.

"How beautiful Venice looks from the sea," Mrs. Hollister remarked, adding, "It's very kind of you to fetch us, Count Gallino."

"It's my pleasure," he replied, "to show you our factory."

Soon the boat reached the island, was moored,

and the visitors stepped out. Their host led them into a long low building.

"First," he said, "I would like to show you how glass is made." He ushered them into a small room in which two men were working. In a corner was a hearth, with a bed of red-hot coals. Over it one man was holding a lump of molten glass on the end of tongs. He withdrew it and gave it to his partner, the glassblower, who fastened the soft glob onto the end of a long tube. With cheeks puffing, he blew and blew, revolving the tube between the palms of his hands.

The Hollisters looked on fascinated as the blob of glass swelled into a long balloon of clear crystal. Then the other man scored a circle about it, tapped one end and broke it off cleanly.

"I see! That's going to be a vase," Holly remarked.

"Or a goblet," Pam said.

The helper set the bowl down carefully and heated another piece over the fire. This the glassblower fashioned into a stem and fused it to the base of the bowl.

"Oh, it *is* a vase!" Pam said to Holly. "And how beautiful!"

When the exhibition was over, Count Gallino escorted his visitors once more into the hallway, mounted four stairs and entered a beautiful display room. The walls were lined with delicate glassware of all kinds and colors.

While the children browsed about the showroom,

Mrs. Hollister selected a lovely red goblet decorated with a gold fleur de lis. She paid the Count for it and gave him Aunt Marge's address in Crestwood, where it was to be sent.

Then the Italian called the others to gather around him. "Now," he said proudly, "I want to show you the most beautiful work in our factory. It is a priceless Madonna, made by the most famous glass artist in Italy. But," he added with a twinkle and a wave of his finger, "it is not for sale, signora. Only to see."

The Hollisters followed the Count toward a small anteroom, and as they did, a man burst out of the doorway, with an excited look on his face. He spoke rapidly in Italian and the Count looked startled. "Stolen? The Madonna stolen?" he exclaimed incredulously.

His employee ran to the window and pointed out over the water. A sleek black craft with a powerful outboard motor was zipping toward the heart of Venice!

The Hollisters watched helplessly while the factory owner called several more employees about him. The Italian words crackled back and forth, punctuated by the Count's sharp orders to his men. When they had all scurried about and disappeared, the Italian pulled a white handkerchief from his breast pocket and mopped his brow.

"I am sorry," he said politely, "but something terrible has happened." He told them that a thief had stolen not only the glass Madonna, but an intricately designed bowl painted with gold leaf, which was considered the most exquisite in all of Venice.

"In broad daylight, too!" he said unhappily. "He must have known exactly where to find those things."

The Count told them that the factory workers had seen the man there several times before. They had thought he was a prospective customer. That morning he had returned, carrying wrapping paper under his coat. It matched the kind with which the glass factory wrapped its parcels.

"The scoundrel walked out as if he had bought some merchandise!" Count Gallino said. "Please excuse me, but I must go to the police. My man will take you back to your hotel."

Before they left, Pete asked for a sample of their wrapping paper. A clerk gave him a piece. It was mocha-colored, with crisscross brown stripes and a light, lettered G every two inches. Pete folded it and put it in his pocket as one of the Count's assistants escorted them back to the boat. Before long they were standing in front of their hotel.

"I wish we could help the Count," Pete said, then added, "Say, what's all the excitement over there?"

Next to the vaporetto wharf a crowd of people had gathered to look at two policemen in a patrol boat and another motorboat alongside it. The boys ran over to see and Ricky beckoned the others to follow.

"It's the getaway boat!" Pete called out. "They've found it already!" There was the same sleek craft they had seen from the factory window. Being careful not to touch any place the thief might have left

107

his fingerprints, the police tied a rope to the front and began towing it away.

"Where did they find it?" asked Holly, trying to see around the people in front of her.

"Right here," said a large lady with an English accent. "It was standing empty. I saw the patrol boat come over for it."

"Then the man must have escaped right about here," Pam said.

"And not too long ago, either," Mrs. Hollister remarked, glancing about her. Suddenly she looked startled. Too excited to speak she squeezed Pete's arm and pointed to the nearby wharf.

Mingling with the crowd about to board a vaporetto was a man carrying two brown packages, one under each arm.

"Do you suppose—?" she asked softly.

"We'll have to find out," Pete said quickly. "Pam, come here! Ricky, follow me!"

"Oh, please be careful," Mrs. Hollister said. "I'll see if I can find a policeman."

Pete, Pam and Ricky ran to the ticket gate, where Pete pulled enough lire from his pocket to pay for three rides. The children jumped onto the vaporetto just as it pulled away from the dock.

"There he is!" Pete said softly. The three made their way through the crowd and stood near the suspect.

On the pretext of looking out over the city, Pete worked his way closer to the man. Now he could see the packages plainly.

The mocha-and-brown paper clearly showed the letters G. No doubt the parcels were from the Count's factory!

Ricky was so excited that he clutched Pam's hand and stared hard at the man. The fellow was tall and thin, with a craggy face and deep-set dark eyes. His coarse brown hair hung long in the back. He wore a white shirt and tan jacket which were neat enough, but his necktie was pulled to one side.

"He looks as if he is in a rush to get somewhere," Ricky whispered to his sister.

As he spoke, Pete made his way back to the others. "I think that's our man, all right," the older boy said.

"What'll we do now?" Pam wondered.

Pete thought for a moment and suggested that perhaps they could crowd about him when he got off the vaporetto, and hold him tightly until they could get help.

"But he looks so strong!" Pam said cautiously.

Listening to the chatter of Italian about them, Pam wished that she could speak the language. "But Pete and I do know how to yell 'help,'" she thought, recalling the note they had found on the Autostrada.

The vaporetto stopped at a station, but the man did not move. At the second stop he looked around nervously and moved toward the exit, but did not get off.

The eyes of the three youngsters never left their quarry. At the next stop the man hefted the package in each arm and pushed his way through the crowd toward the exit.

"Stick close!" Pete told Pam and Ricky.

As the fellow stepped off the boat, Pete slipped through the milling passengers, threw his arms about the man and cried "Halt!"

Pam and Ricky did the same. The fellow was so startled they could feel his body tense up as they clung to him. He dropped one package and Pete let go of him to catch it.

Wrenching himself clear of the other children, the thief dashed off.

"Help! *Aiuto!*" Pam shouted

The onlookers seemed to be as startled as the fugitive and did nothing. Pete thrust the parcel into Pam's arms. "Take this to the police," he said, and raced off after the fugitive.

Across the boat landing and down a narrow alley Pete ran. He could see the thief's brown hair bobbing up and down some distance ahead.

Pete's legs flew fast over the cobbled pavement. The man was still in sight! Suddenly he turned a corner into a smaller alley. Pete had to skid to a stop to make the turn. He was just in time to see the fleeing figure slip into a doorway with a hotel sign over it.

Now the boy advanced cautiously. He looked inside to see a small shabby office and a gray-haired man standing by a key rack behind a counterr. "Hello," Pete said. "Did you just see a man come in here?"

"Ah, *Americano*," the clerk replied. "You wish to see Signor Olevi?"

Pete gulped. "Yes."

"Room 205," the man said, pointing up the stairs with a motion of his thumb. "A small hotel," he added with a shrug. "No elevator."

Pete went up the steps two at a time and proceeded along a hallway at the end of which was a window looking down on a canal. "Room 203—204—" Pete said to himself. "That must be 205 at the end of the corridor." Suddenly he stopped short. The door was ajar. He approached on tiptoe, not daring to make a sound.

Putting his fingertips against the door, Pete pushed it open a little more. He listened.

No sound.

He peered inside, but the small room seemed to be empty. Against the wall beneath a window was a cot. Across the room was a dresser, a desk and a wooden chair.

With pulses racing, Pete held his breath and took one step inside. Where had the fugitive gone? Had he left any clue to—

Crash! A man leaped from behind the door, bowling Pete head over heels. Then the fellow, carrying the brown package and a small suitcase, dashed out of the door and slammed it shut. The key turned in the lock. Pete was a prisoner!

CHAPTER 11

BOLD ESCAPE

DAZED by the collision, Pete picked himself off the floor and tugged at the doorknob. He could only rattle it, but no more! Scolding himself for walking into the trap, the boy hastened to the window and looked out. Two stories below was the brownish water of a small canal. But at the moment no boats were in sight.

"I'll call the concierge," he told himself. He looked around the room for a telephone. There was none.

"I must get out of here quickly," Pete thought, "or else the thief will make a clean getaway."

The boy banged on the door for a few minutes without any luck. Then he went to the cot, tore off the two sheets and knotted them together. He tied one end to the bureau and threw the trailing part out the window, where it hung down alongside the building nearly to the water's edge.

Pete watched and soon saw the nose of a gondola coming slowly around the bend in the canal.

"Gondolier!" the boy shouted. Then he eased

himself out the window and began to shin down the sheet rope.

Seeing what was happening, the oarsman quickened his strokes and pulled alongside the building. Pete dropped into the boat, gave the name of his hotel, and said, "Hurry! Fast! *Pronto!*"

The gondolier, a sturdy middle-aged man wearing a bandana around his brow, set off at a brisk clip, bobbing back and forth as he pressed his weight against the oar. Soon they were in the Grand Canal, where the boatman wove in and out of water traffic as he headed toward the Doges' Palace.

As soon as the gondola touched the dock, Pete thanked the man, paid his fare, jumped ashore and raced to the hotel. There he found the rest of his family in agitated conversation with two policemen.

"Thank heavens, there you are!" Mrs. Hollister exclaimed. "What happened?"

While Pete quickly told of his capture and escape, one of the officers, who spoke English, took notes. When the story was finished, Pete turned to Pam. "How did you and Ricky get back?"

His sister said that they had returned to the hotel by vaporetto, called the police and given them the package.

"It was the beautiful bowl," said the officer and thanked Pete warmly for its return.

"But the thief still has the glass Madonna," the boy said.

The officer said they would go at once to the man's hotel to look for clues.

"And it's high time we had lunch," Mrs. Hollister declared as the policemen departed.

While they were eating their late meal in an open-air café, Pete asked permission to take Pam and return to the thief's hotel. "I'd like to find out more about him if I can, Mother."

Mrs. Hollister looked doubtful.

"The police will probably still be there," Pam put in, "so we'll be safe."

With a warning to be careful, their mother gave her consent and the two children set off in a vaporetto. Half an hour later they were walking along the cobbled alley which led to the small hotel. They entered and confronted the concierge.

"I'd like to pay you for wrinkling two sheets," Pete said.

The gray-haired man declined and said nervously, "The police have just left. They informed me of your brave escape and I told them all I knew of this fellow Olevi."

"Can you tell us too?" Pam asked politely.

The clerk said that four men had taken the room a little over a month before. For the last three weeks, however, only Olevi had used it. "Yesterday one of them came back—a little man with a mustache. I didn't know the names of the others," he said.

"May we search the room?" asked Pete.

"Please, children," said the man kindly, "don't bother me any more. I have had too much excitement for today."

114

Pete and Pam said they were sorry and left the hotel. Disappointed, they retraced their steps until they came to a small souvenir shop two doors away.

Looking at the postcards in the window reminded both children of the card from Giovanni.

"We ought to go in and ask if they've seen him," Pam remarked.

"Okay," her brother replied, "but I don't think it's any use. There must be hundreds of card shops in Venice."

"This is an out-of-the-way street," Pam said thoughtfully. "It would be a good neighborhood to hide someone in."

They entered the shop.

Behind the counter was a very short stout woman with bright black eyes. Pete pulled the picture of Giovanni Boschi from his pocket and showed it to her.

"Do you speak English?"

"A leetle."

"Have you ever seen this man?" the boy asked.

"Sì, sì."

The children stared at her, unable to believe their ears.

"What did you say?" Pam asked.

"Sì—yes," repeated the woman firmly. In halting English she told them that the old gentleman had bought a postcard, scribbled something on it, left a hundred lire and quickly slipped out of her store.

"About a month ago?" Pete asked.

"Sì, sì." Now her dark eyes snapped with excitement. "Then they grab him," she said loudly.

"Who?" chorused the children.

"Men," she replied, and held up two fingers.

"Do you know where they took him?" Pete asked eagerly.

With a sweep of her arm the shopkeeper pointed toward the hotel. "That way," she said.

"I'll bet Giovanni was trying to escape!" Pete declared. "Let's go back to the hotel, Pam."

"To search the room?"

"Right. Maybe there's a connection between the Boschi case and the thieves." They thanked the woman and hurried out.

The concierge was surprised to see the Hollisters back again.

"Excuse us," said Pete, "but this is important." He showed the picture of Giovanni Boschi. "Was this one of your guests?"

The hotel keeper shook his head no. He remembered seeing a fifth man go in and out, but had never got a good look at the fellow's face.

"It could have been Giovanni!" Pam thought.

"May we examine the room, please?" Pete requested earnestly.

"We won't bother you," Pam promised.

"Here's the key," the clerk said, "but the police have searched it already."

Pete and Pam hastened upstairs, unlocked the door and entered the room. The cot had been remade and the place was neat. Pete looked in the wastebasket. It had been emptied. A search of the drawers and the closet revealed nothing.

Pam looked through the desk again. There were several envelopes and sheets of white writing paper bearing the hotel's name. The girl was about to shut the drawer when she noticed the faintest of shadows on the white paper.

"I think I've found something," she said. Pam took the top paper from the pile, went to the window and held it up to the light.

"Crickets!" Pete said. "This sheet was underneath one which someone wrote on. The pressure from the pencil shows right through." Pam tilted the paper to see the indentations more clearly.

"It looks like the plan of a house or building," she remarked. Then she read the words *"Firenze Pitti."*

"Something to do with the city of Florence!" Pete said excitedly.

"And that's where Giovanni's puppets were on sale!" Pam exclaimed. "Oh Pete, these thieves must have kidnaped Giovanni!"

"We've got to go to Florence," Pete declared as Pam gave him the paper. "They may be holding him there now!"

"Let's hurry back and tell mother," said Pam. "There's no time to waste."

Leaving the hotel, Pete glanced up the street in time to see a small, dark-haired man step quickly into a doorway. The boy gripped Pam's hand and said, "Walk fast. I think we're being watched."

"It looks like the plan of a building."

Half running, they made their way through the narrow streets to the vaporetto. When they finally reached their own hotel, both children paused and looked around. The dark man was not in sight.

With sighs of relief, they hastened inside. At the desk the concierge handed Pete a note from Mrs. Hollister. It said that she and the others had gone shopping and would return shortly.

While waiting, Pam asked the concierge about the word *Pitti*. She was told that the Pitti Palace was a world-famous museum in Florence.

Pete thanked the man and drew Pam into the comfortable hotel parlor, where they sat side by side on a sofa. "I'll bet these crooks plan to rob the Pitti Palace," the boy said.

"Maybe they specialize in stealing art work," Pam suggested, then added, "but why would they be holding Giovanni?"

"Where is more important than why," her brother replied. A moment later he jumped up. "I've got an idea!" Pam followed him to the telephone booth near the desk where he looked up the number of an American newspaper service. From the reporter in charge he learned that the store in Florence where the puppets had been sold was called Valerio's. Pete reported this to his sister.

"We'll start our search right there," declared Pam.

Just then Mrs. Hollister, Ricky, Holly and Sue bustled into the hotel.

Before Pete and Pam could tell their news, Holly

burst out, "We had a wonderful time shopping!" She was holding an armful of packages.

"And we got some free, too," Sue piped up.

"We went to Count Gallino's factory again," Ricky put in.

Mrs. Hollister told her older children that the Count had come to call for them. "He thanks you for your part in saving the priceless crystal bowl," she said, "and gave presents to all of us."

"We haven't opened them yet," said Holly. "Come on!" She hastened into the parlor and they unwrapped the gifts on a marble-topped table. Sue received a glass baby deer. Ricky had a Pekingese dog and Holly a Siamese cat. Pam opened her gift, to find a solid glass goldfish of exquisite beauty; Pete's was a knight on horseback.

"How sweet of the Count!" Pam declared as she rewrapped her gift carefully in tissue.

"We have some surprises too," Pete said, and told the others about the clues they had found and where they thought Giovanni was.

"You are right," said their mother. "We *must* go to Florence."

"When?" Ricky asked, making his dog prance from one armchair to another. "This afternoon?"

Mrs. Hollister glanced at Pete and Pam.

"Crickets, that would be great," her son replied.

"I'll make a hotel reservation right away," said Mrs. Hollister.

An hour later the family was at the huge parking garage with all their baggage. Holly was carrying a bag of sweet rolls they had bought to eat on the way. They had decided to have late supper when they reached Florence.

Mrs. Hollister drove out of the garage, recrossed the causeway and went through several towns before Holly, kneeling on the back seat, noticed something strange. "There's a little red car that's been following us," she told her mother.

While she spoke, they were approaching a narrow bridge which carried the road over a small stream.

Suddenly the red auto put on a burst of speed.

"He's trying to pass us!" Pete said. "Look out, Mother!"

The car drew alongside and Pam let out a cry of fright. The driver was the thief they had followed on the vaporetto! A man, seated beside him, was short and had a dark mustache.

The red car pulled ahead until its back end was even with the front of the Hollisters' car. Then the driver edged Mrs. Hollister closer to the side of the road. Straight ahead was the stone abutment of the bridge.

"Mommy," Sue screamed. "We're going to hit it!"

CHAPTER 12

A FUNNY BRIDGE

As THE children gasped, Mrs. Hollister pulled as far to the side of the road as she could. She slowed the car carefully and came to a halt only a few inches from the bridge abutment.

"Mommy, you're great!" Holly declared. "I want to grow up to be a lady driver like you!"

By the time Mrs. Hollister backed up and drove on across the bridge, the red car was out of sight.

For a few miles everyone was quiet, thinking about the near-accident. Then Pete spoke up. "We must have found some very valuable information, Mother," the boy said. "Those crooks don't want us to go on any further."

"But we will just the same!" declared Ricky.

"That's right," his mother said. "We'll not let anyone frighten us off."

Soon afterward the road widened into a superhighway. It led across rugged mountainous country with breath-taking scenery. Bridges, viaducts and tunnels curved and dipped through pine-clad hills, where once Roman armies had marched north to meet ancient invaders.

The youngsters were so fascinated by the ride that they took no note of the passing time. Finally, at dusk, the road opened into a valley many miles wide, and off to the left they could see the twinkling lights of the city of Florence.

Mrs. Hollister drove carefully to the center of town, asked questions of a policeman and easily found their hotel.

When they had placed the bags in their rooms they gathered in the lobby. Pete telephoned the local police department to report the Pitti Palace clue they had found in Venice.

"Thank you," the officer said in good English. "But I am afraid your clue comes too late." He told Pete that a valuable painting had been stolen from the art museum the night before.

"We found fingerprints," the officer went on, "and they match ones found by the Venice police after the theft of the glass Madonna."

Pete then told all about the Hollister's part in the strange case. "We're going to look for Giovanni Boschi here," Pete said.

"Good, but be careful," came the reply.

When the others heard the police report they were excited.

"I was right!" Pam said. "This *is* a gang of art thieves!"

But no one could fathom why they would be holding Nada's uncle prisoner. "He knows something, I'll bet," Pete said. "And they've kidnaped him so he can't tell the police."

The Hollisters dined at the hotel, retired and rose early next morning to the sound of traffic noises from the street beneath their windows.

"Let's visit Valerio's first thing," Pete suggested at the breakfast table.

From the desk clerk they learned that Valerio's was on a bridge called Ponte Vecchio across the Arno River.

"Yikes! A store on a bridge?" Ricky asked.

The clerk smiled down at the youngster. "There is no traffic on it any more," he replied. "Only shops."

"Thank you," Pam said. "I'm sure we can find it."

The family set out along the narrow streets, lined with fruit and vegetable stalls, restaurants and stores of all kinds. Soon they came to an avenue hugging the bank of the Arno River. The children looked down into the water. It was mud-brown and moved swiftly.

"Oh, look at the odd boats," Pam remarked as two scullers, their oars sweeping back and forth like long spider legs, skimmed upstream. They disappeared for a moment under the strangest bridge the children had ever seen. It looked like a city block on low arches. Shops lined both sides of the ancient span.

Careful to avoid the cars and motor scooters whizzing past, the children hastened to the bridge and walked out on it. Valerio's was near the center. It sold art work, leather goods, jewelry and dolls.

Mrs. Hollister walked into the open door, followed by her children. A stout man greeted them cheerfully and introduced himself as Mr. Valerio. "What would you like to see?" he asked.

"We're here on a mission," Mrs. Hollister replied, then turned to Pam. "You be the spokesman for us, dear."

The girl unfolded their part in the story of Giovanni Boschi's disappearance. When she had finished, she asked, "Do you have any more of the Punch puppets, Mr. Valerio?"

"Just one." He called a girl clerk and spoke in Italian. She disappeared into the back of the shop and returned with a flat white box. The shopkeeper opened it. Inside lay one Punch puppet.

"That's an original, all right!" Pete exclaimed. "Look at the mole on Punch's nose."

Pam picked up the doll and examined it carefully. She slid her fingers inside the head. Nothing there.

"I guess the police have seen this, too," Pete said.

"Not this one," replied Mr. Valerio. "I came across it after I had given the other boxes of puppets to the police."

Now Pete questioned the cordial shopkeeper about the person who had sold him the Punches.

"He was not a regular salesman," the shopkeeper replied. "I had not seen him before and have not seen him since." He described the man as short, thin and sharp-faced.

"May I examine this box, please?" Pam asked.

"Help yourself."

Pam looked at the cover. It was plain, with no markings on it. The inside gave no hint of its origin, either. Then she turned it upside down.

"Oh, look!" she exclaimed. In a corner was a scrawled profile of Punch and beside it some Italian words.

"Yikes!" Ricky cried. "That's a message from Giovanni!"

Mr. Valerio bent close to see.

"What does it say?" Pam asked.

The stout man shook his head. "There are eight words here, but the meaning of the message I do not know." He translated. "Glass Gallino. Painting Pitti. Marble Rome. Shell Caramagna."

"It's a list of the robbers' plans," declared Pam.

Even Mr. Valerio grew excited as he heard the young sleuths make their deductions. Glass already had been stolen from the Gallino factory in Venice. And only night before last the painting had disappeared from the Pitti Palace.

"Then you mean," Mr. Valerio asked, "that something marble will be stolen from Rome, and a shell from someone or someplace named Caramagna?"

"That's exactly the way we have it figured," Ricky said seriously. "And we'll catch those crooks yet!"

The shopkeeper shook his head incredulously. "I can't believe it," he said, "that you children can solve a case like this."

He wrapped the Punch doll separately and Mrs.

"Where else can we look for Punch puppets?"

Hollister paid for it. Then Pam took the box under her arm. They thanked Mr. Valerio for his help and started to leave. Holly turned back and twirled a pigtail. "Where else can we look for Punch puppets, Mr. Valerio?" she asked.

"Crickets!" Pete declared. "I never thought to ask that question!"

"Yes," came the reply. "My friend Muro in Pisa bought some, too."

After thanking the man again, they left.

"Yikes! What clues!" Ricky said, amazed.

"What shall we do next?" Pete asked as they retraced their steps across the bridge.

It was decided they should take the white box to the police. "Otherwise no one will believe this story," Pam said, observing the eight words written in ink.

"They can tell the police in Rome to be on the lookout," was Pete's suggestion.

"And how about poor Mr. Caramagna?" Holly said. "We should tell him too."

"Right," said Pete. "His factory is marked for a robbery. I think we should inform him right now."

Pete hastened back to Valerio's. There the kind shopkeeper telephoned long distance to Mr. Caramagna's cameo factory.

"Here," the man said, passing the telephone to Pete. "This employee speaks English."

Pete found himself on the line with a Mr. Nitto, who said he was the owner's private secretary. When Pete had given his information, the man on the other end laughed loudly. "You are a boy?" he asked. "How old?"

"Twelve," Pete replied.

"And you expect me to believe this wild story?"

"I know it's strange," Pete said, "but it's true. Please let me speak to Mr. Caramagna. He knows me," the boy added, and explained how he had met the factory owner in Milan.

Mr. Nitto said that his employer could not be disturbed. "He's working on a very important job."

Pete pleaded, but he could not persuade Mr. Nitto to let him speak with the factory owner.

"Please," said Pete to Mr. Valerio, "you try."

The shopkeeper took over the phone, spoke firmly in Italian. He listened a moment, then hung up.

"I'm sorry," he said to the boy. "He did not believe me, either." Mr. Valerio would not allow Pete to pay for the call, and wished him well. The downhearted sleuth left the shop and reported to the others.

"If we take this box to the police I'm sure they can convince Mr. Nitto," Pam said.

The family walked along the bridge, and when they reached the end, a crowd of jolly sight-seers came rollicking past. One boy, about sixteen, accidently bumped into Pam. The white box flew from her hands and over the side of the bridge, down toward the Arno River.

CHAPTER 13

THE TOWER OF PISA

THE flat box zigzagged and dipped like a kite without a string, finally landing in the muddy waters of the river.

"We must get it!" Pam cried out as the children raced to the narrow sidewalk bordering the Arno. They watched the current carry the box downstream. But at the same time they saw a lone sculler bending to his oars not far from the floating clue.

Pete cupped his hands and called out, "Help! *Aiuto!*" with all his might. The other children echoed him and the rower heard them. He turned in his seat, and when he saw that they were pointing to the floating box, he grasped it as it came past. With a wave of his hand, he motioned to a spot down river where the children could reach the water level.

Sculling quickly to the spot, the Italian youth skimmed the water-soaked box onto the shore, then with a grin set off again. Nimble Ricky was the first to reach the place. He picked up the box and gave it to Pam. The girl turned it over quickly to look at the writing.

The ink had run! The message had disappeared!

Now Pam looked crestfallen. Who would believe their story, she thought, without seeing proof of Giovanni Boschi's message?

Climbing up onto the roadway again, the girl dropped the sodden box into a trash can. "Crickets!" Pete said. "One of our best clues—gone."

After a hasty conference among the five children and their mother, it was decided that they should set off for Pisa immediately. In forty minutes they were on their way. Pete and Pam had read about the famous Leaning Tower, and all were eager to see it.

The road, narrow and winding, led westward through low, hilly farmland studded with small villages. The houses were so close to the road that the travelers could see through the curtains of red, blue and green cords which hung in the doorways. Sometimes brown-eyed smiling children peeked out to wave at the passing car.

After several hours the family reached the outskirts of Pisa. From there Mrs. Hollister followed signs leading through the city streets to the Leaning Tower.

At last they came to a river and crossed the bridge into a green meadow. Before them lay a lovely church. Behind it rose a tall tower, leaning slightly.

"Look out, Mommy!" Sue warned as they drove closer. "It's going to fall over!"

"No it's not," said Pete.

"We hope," added Ricky.

Mrs. Hollister parked the car directly in front of the souvenir shop bearing the name Muro. But a card on the door told them it was closed for lunch.

The family decided they would eat, too, do some sight-seeing and return. They entered a small restaurant near by and had a tasty meal of spaghetti and roasted chicken.

As soon as they were finished, Ricky pushed his chair back from the table. "Come on," he said impatiently. "I want to climb that goofy tower."

Outside, the children ran and skipped along the sidewalk until they reached the entrance to the Tower of Pisa. Holding hands, Sue and Holly led the way to a ticket-seller at the foot of the stone steps.

After Mrs. Hollister had paid the man a small fee, the visitors climbed up the winding stairway. At the second landing they stopped to walk out on the sloping ledge which encircled the structure.

"Come back, Sue," Pam called, grabbing her little sister. "Don't go near the edge." Even Ricky was a little frightened and backtracked up the stone slope to go inside again. Then up they went once more, round and round, until they reached the observation tower at the top.

Below them, surrounding the church buildings and shops, lay green and gold fields of farmland.

"Is it going to fall?"

As Pete looked down at the street he saw a man approach the front door of Muro's store, unlock it and walk inside. But before the boy had a chance to mention this, a frightening thing happened.

A deep rumbling filled the air and the tower shook!

Other visitors cried out in alarm and a woman screamed, "Earthquake!" The rumbling kept up for a few seconds and the leaning tower shook with a sickening spasm. Everyone raced for the stone steps and began to clatter down them. Despite the headlong rush, all the tourists managed to get out with only a few bumps and bruises.

The street was in an uproar, and police arrived quickly to rope off a large area around the tower.

"Is it going to fall?" asked Ricky, looking up.

"No damage seems to be done this time," an Italian man replied, "but we fear that some day we may lose our beautiful campanile."

As the Hollisters walked back to Muro's store, the children's mother explained that builders had begun the tower hundreds of years ago. It settled to one side. "Work was stopped on it for a long time," she said. "Finally the stone masonry was completed."

As she spoke, they reached the door of the souvenir shop. The window glass was cracked, and the proprietor was patching it with tape.

When the Hollisters explained their mission, Mr. Muro greeted them with handshakes.

"I am happy to hear from my friend Valerio,"

he said, then added, "I am sorry, but my Punch puppets are all sold. However, I have other dolls. Would you like to see them?"

"No, thank you," Pam replied. "We wanted this special Pulcinello." Then an idea popped into her head. "Do you have the box they came in?"

"Perhaps, in my basement."

While Mrs. Hollister, Ricky, Holly and Sue looked around the souvenir shop, Pete and Pam accompanied the proprietor down a flight of sturdy wooden steps. Neatly stacked against one wall were boxes of many sizes.

Mr. Muro looked through them all with the help of the two children. "It was a white one, I remember," the shopkeeper said. "No, it's gone. I must have used it."

Back up in the shop, Pete asked what the puppet-seller had looked like. Mr. Muro's description fitted the short thin man Mr. Valerio had seen.

"The fellow had a Neopolitan manner of speaking," the shopkeeper added.

"How do you mean?" asked Holly. She was told that some people living in Naples clip off the ends of their words.

"A short thin man from Naples," said Pete. "That's not much to go on."

During the conversation, Mrs. Hollister had been holding several tiny silver models of the Tower of Pisa.

"Mommy's going to send these back to Shoreham for Ann and Donna," Sue said happily.

When the purchases were made, the Hollisters thanked the shopkeeper and returned to their car. There they decided to drive as far as possible that evening, stay overnight somewhere, and proceed to Rome next day.

"Before we leave Pisa," said Pete, "I think Mother should try calling Mr. Caramagna." Mrs. Hollister agreed, got out of the car and went into a nearby store to phone.

When she returned she shook her head. "No use," she said, slipping behind the wheel. "I got Mr. Nitto, and he didn't believe me, either."

Ricky turned red. "He's got some nerve."

"Perhaps in Rome we can fit our clues and Nada's together," Pam said, "and come closer to solving the mystery."

"If we can't get in touch with Mr. Caramagna by phone," Pete spoke up, "we'll have to go warn him personally."

Mrs. Hollister guided the car out of Pisa and took the road west. When they reached the Tyrrhenian seacoast, they stopped for a few minutes to gaze out over the blue water. Then they drove southward until they came to the town of Grosseto. There they spent the night in a hotel.

Early next morning, Mrs. Hollister arranged for hotel reservations in Rome. Then, after a hearty breakfast, the family was on its way again.

"See how the countryside is changing," Pam said as they rode through a wide plain which sloped gently to the sea. Broad wheatfields on either side of the highway were sprinkled with orange poppies.

Finally at a crossroads several miles north of Rome, Mrs. Hollister stopped for gasoline. As the attendant filled the tank, Pam said to her mother, "Let's call Nada now and tell her we're coming."

"That's a good idea," Mrs. Hollister said. The gas station attendant, who spoke a little English, put the call through. "Here's your number," he said.

Pam took the telephone. "Hello, Nada? Is this you? It's Pam Hollister."

The voice at the other end was a man's. He spoke English with a heavy accent. "Nada has left a message for you," he said. "Her Uncle Giovanni has been found and all is well."

"Oh, how wonderful!" Pam cried with delight. "And may I ask who you are, please?"

"I am Nada's father," came the reply.

CHAPTER 14

THE NIGHT PATROL

"Nada's father?" said Pam. "Oh. Good-by."

"What were you talking about?" Mrs. Hollister asked as her daughter hung up the phone. "Nada's father is not living."

"That's just it, Mother!" Pam said, agitated. "There's some man in Nada's house pretending to be her father." She told what the fellow had said.

"It's all a lie," declared Pete.

"What can we do about it?" asked Ricky as they walked back to their car.

"We'd better get to Rome and find Nada as fast as we can," his brother replied.

On the way into the city the travelers worried about what might have happened to the Italian girl and her mother.

"Maybe someone's out to kidnap them, too," Holly suggested.

Pam did not think anybody would be as mean as all that. Yet, something very strange was going on and the Hollisters were determined to find out what.

With Pete reading the map, his mother drove into the teeming, bustling city of Rome.

"Yikes!" Ricky said. "Some traffic!" Cars, mostly small ones, seemed to come at them from all directions, but Mrs. Hollister was not frightened.

Finally they drove onto a beautiful tree-lined avenue which curved up a hill. Set back from the broad sidewalks were large hotels.

"There, I see ours!" Pam said, and her mother pulled up in front of an older, comfortable-looking building.

As soon as they were registered and the luggage settled in their rooms, the family returned to the car. Pete checked the map of Rome to locate the Boschis' apartment. Then they set off through traffic again.

Mrs. Hollister nearly entered a one-way street in the wrong direction, but a quick flick of the wheel set them right again. Horns honked, the hot sun beat down, and the tangle of cars grew so thick that for several minutes the Hollisters' vehicle could only crawl along.

"Nada's street should be the next one to the right," Pete said finally. It proved to be in a quiet residential section of gracious old apartment houses, tan-colored, with carved marble columns beside the doorways. Mrs. Hollister parked at the proper number and they got out.

"Do you think we should take a policeman with us?" Ricky asked as they approached the entrance. The others thought not. Perhaps Nada had a new father now. What then? Everyone would be terribly embarrassed.

The heavy front door opened to Pete's sturdy push, as did the inner one leading to a flight of steps. Pam's quick glance had noted the apartment number on a list in the vestibule.

Quietly the family mounted the marble stairway to the third floor landing. The name Boschi was printed in bold, black letters over the doorbell of the first apartment.

"Yikes," Ricky said. "What'll we do if this man jumps out at us?"

"Don't worry," Pete replied. "We could grab him." He took a deep breath and pushed the buzzer.

"Somebody's coming," whispered Sue, as they heard light footsteps.

Mrs. Hollister and her children stepped back and the door opened quietly. There stood little Nada! She gasped in surprise when she saw them.

"The Hollisters!" she squealed. "Mother! Come!"

Mrs. Boschi hurried to the door and hugged her callers. "Why didn't you telephone us?" she asked. "We'd have come to your hotel."

The Americans were ushered into a tastefully decorated living room, hung with colorful pictures. A small statuette of the Madonna stood on an end table, reminding Pam of the theft in Venice.

"Oh, Mrs. Boschi, Nada," she said, "so much has happened since we came to Italy!"

"Have you learned any more about my uncle?" Nada asked.

"Yes," said Pete, "but first we must tell you

something else. When we called you up this morning, a man answered the phone."

"Impossible!" said Mrs. Boschi. "No man has been here."

"He said he was Nada's father," Pam carried on.

At this the Italian dress designer paled. "That is terrible!" she said, and Nada began to weep softly.

Sue went over to the Italian girl, wriggled on her lap and put an arm around Nada's neck. "We'll catch the bad man!" she whispered.

Pam felt like crying too when she saw how their Roman friends were affected.

Mrs. Boschi explained that they had been out visiting for several hours that morning. "Someone must have entered our apartment," she said, "but I can't understand why."

"To look for something," was Pete's guess.

The Italian woman said that nothing had been disturbed so far as she had noticed.

"You ought to make a good search," Pam suggested.

With everyone watching, Nada and her mother examined all the drawers and the closets. Nothing seemed to be missing.

"What's this?" Pete asked finally, bending down to look at an old wooden chest in the corner of the coat closet.

"That belongs to Uncle Giovanni," Mrs. Boschi said. "He keeps his private papers and old trinkets in it."

"May I examine it?"

"This has been ransacked!"

"Of course."

Pete tried the lid but the box was locked.

"You see, it hasn't been touched," Mrs. Boschi said.

"You'd better open it anyhow if you can," Pete said. "There might be a clue inside."

The woman got the key from her top left dresser drawer, gave it to Pete, and he inserted it into the lock. *Click!*

When the boy lifted the lid, he cried out in surprise. "What a mess! This has been ransacked." He and Ricky pulled the box out of the closet, and the excited Mrs. Boschi looked through the contents.

She pulled out the original model of the Punch puppet, some old newspaper clippings and legal papers. Then she drew in her breath sharply and looked up at the children. "Uncle Giovanni's passport! It's gone!"

"That's bad," Pete said. "With it, they can take your uncle out of Italy."

The young sleuths deduced that Giovanni Boschi's captors had forced him to tell where he kept the passport and the key to the chest. "They probably watched your apartment," Pam said, "and when you went out, they entered with a passkey."

"Then Pam called up," Mrs. Hollister put in, "and the prowler answered the phone."

All agreed that this was a case for the police. They were summoned and arrived a few minutes later. The three officers were told what had happened. One man, who had a fingerprint kit, set about dusting objects which the intruder might have touched, but he found no prints except those of the Boschis. The prowler probably had used gloves.

Before the policemen left, Pete told them everything that the Hollisters had discovered about Giovanni and the thieves. He concluded with the washed-out clue on the box in Florence.

"Would you please warn the cameo factory?" Pete requested. "They'll believe you."

One of the policemen went to the phone and quickly put through the call. He spoke rapidly in Italian for a few minutes, listened, looked satisfied and hung up.

"Signor Caramagna was not there," he reported, "but I told his secretary, Mr. Nitto."

The children looked disappointed.

"Don't worry," said the officer with a smile. "He has promised to take every precaution."

Holly spoke up. "What about 'Marble—Rome?'"

The officer pondered. "Not much to go on," he said, but promised to notify the Vigili Notturni dell'Urbe.

"What's that?" Ricky wanted to know.

They were told that the Vigili was a force of six hundred bicycle policemen who patrolled the streets of Rome by night.

"If I got lost, could they find me?" asked Sue, balancing on one foot.

"Sì, sì—even such a tiny signorina!" On this jolly note the police left, but the seriousness of the mystery remained, even during luncheon, which

144

Mrs. Boschi prepared for everyone. While they were eating, Nada said, "Even though you don't have to worry about Signor Caramagna anymore, you ought to visit Pompeii."

"We'll do that tomorrow," said Mrs. Hollister, and her children exchanged delighted grins.

That afternoon both families went sight-seeing. Since the Boschis had another engagement for dinner, they said good-by to the Hollisters in front of their hotel. "Good luck on your trip," the Italian woman said.

"Please let us know if you learn anything more about Uncle Giovanni," Nada added, and the girls kissed.

As she walked away with her mother, Nada called back, "You're all wonderful detectives."

"She's not bad for a girl," Ricky remarked as he went into the lobby.

The family rested for a while, then dined late. As they left the restaurant Mrs. Hollister said, "I have one more surprise for you."

"What, Mother?" Holly asked eagerly.

"To see the Coliseum by moonlight," she replied.

"The ancient Roman arena!" Pete exclaimed. "Crickets! That'll be great!"

They squeezed into a taxi, sitting on one another's laps. As they drove along, another cab kept close behind. When Pete noticed this, he told his mother.

"But Rome is full of taxis," she said. "Look, we're following one too!"

The driver let them off in front of the Coliseum. The children looked up at the huge broken wall, rising in tiers of arches.

"Oh," said Pam, "it must have been magnificent!"

As the Hollisters went through the entrance, they passed only a few people going in and out.

Holding hands, the family walked up to the edge of a vast pit in the center of the stadium. The great ruin was ghostly in the moonlight.

Suddenly, halfway out of the shadows, stepped a man. The children saw only part of his thin, sharp face. "My advice," he hissed, "is for you to leave Rome!"

CHAPTER 15

AN ODD MOVE

THE fellow darted back into the shadows, and another man emerged. "You are confused with the Coliseum?" he asked. This strange question, coming on top of the threat, was too much for Pete.

"Confused!" the boy exclaimed. "I'll say we are —about this whole mystery."

"Mystery?" the man asked, stepping farther out into the moonlight. "Ah yes, the Coliseum *is* a mystery, for there are many questions which tourists like answered. May I help you?" From his pocket he pulled a card. It proved that he was a qualified and official guide. "One of many," he said, "in the city of Rome."

"Yes, you may help us," Mrs. Hollister replied. She pointed into the great pit in the floor of the arena. "Those look like old cellars. Is that what they are?"

The guide told them that during the days of Rome's glory, the Coliseum had a lake in the middle of it. Then, after the city had fallen, the lake was drained by the inhabitants, who put up houses where the water had been. "Those are the remains of the old dwellings," he said.

As the Hollisters listened, the guide gave many other interesting facts about the Coliseum. It had been built, they learned, by fifteen thousand slaves captured in Jerusalem. "Thousands died during the construction," he said, "and when the moon shines, like tonight, I feel as if their ghosts are roaming here."

Pete chuckled and said, "That's all we need now. A few assorted ghosts to add to our puzzle."

By this time little Sue was so tired that she climbed into her mother's arms. As the guide pointed out the barred cages where the lions had been kept, Sue whispered, "Lions are big pussies," and fell asleep.

Their tour over, Mrs. Hollister thanked the guide, paid him for his services and led her family out of the Coliseum. Several taxis waited at the curb. Before entering one of them, the youngsters looked about carefully, but could see no one who appeared to be following.

Back at the hotel, they found a bellboy dozing behind the desk. Sleepily, he gave Pete the key, and the family took the elevator to their two-room suite. Pete unlocked one of the doors and they entered. Instantly they knew something was wrong.

"Our baggage is gone!" Holly cried out. Pam rushed to the clothes closet. There was not a garment left. Holly began to wail, which wakened Sue, still asleep in her mother's arms.

"We've been robbed!"

Frightened, the little girl cried out, "Save me from the lions!"

During the commotion, Pam telephoned to the desk. But the bellman could not understand what she was saying because of the noise. A few minutes later he rushed into the room. "I can explain, I can explain!" he said.

"We've been robbed, that's what!" Pete declared hotly.

"I can explain," the boy insisted. When the distraught family quieted, he told them that their suite had been reserved for another client several weeks before. "So we moved you into other quarters," the embarrassed bellman declared.

"Why didn't you tell us?" asked Holly.

He said that a notice of the change had been left in the Hollisters' mailbox. He had been too sleepy, however, to remember to give it to them.

Mrs. Hollister heaved a great sigh of relief, and the family followed the clerk to their new rooms farther down the hall.

After their day of excitement, falling asleep was easy; so easy, in fact, that Ricky flopped on his bed without undressing. Pete removed his brother's shoes and helped him strip off his shirt, as the redhead bobbed drowsily from side to side.

When the sun streamed into their windows the next morning, the boys rubbed their eyes sleepily. As soon as Pete became fully awake he telephoned to the police station. Had the bicycle cops found anybody trying to steal a marble statue? The news he received was disappointing. No thief had been caught. But a famous small marble statue had been stolen!

"They got away with it!" Pete exclaimed, pounding a fist into his hand. "And the cameo factory is next!"

In a few minutes Mrs. Hollister and the girls were sitting on their beds in bathrobes, listening to Pete's report.

"Why worry?" Holly asked. "Mr. Caramagna has been warned."

"How do we know Mr. Nitto gave him the message?" Pete replied, then he added, "Mother, I have the strongest feeling that we ought to warn Mr. Caramagna ourselves."

Pam agreed. "Three of the four thefts have taken place this week," she said in a worried voice. "The last one may be scheduled for today."

"Yikes," Ricky said, "we'd better hurry!"

"We'll go as soon as we've had breakfast," declared Mrs. Hollister. With bags finally packed and in the car, the family set off once more. Pete read the map, trying to guide his mother south through the city and onto the road leading to Pompeii. But after quite a while, they were still threading their way through Roman traffic.

"Wait, Mother," Pete said finally. "I think we have taken the wrong turn." Mrs. Hollister pulled up to a curb, and Pete asked a passerby for directions. He could not speak English!

They drove on farther and stopped again. "Do you speak English?" Pete asked a man.

"Yes, I'm a Scot." The visitor said he had arrived only yesterday. "Sorry I can't direct you," he said. "I can't even find my own hotel!"

Up one street and down another, they rode anxiously. Finally, they came onto a broad highway and followed it.

It was Pam who made the discovery. "Mother!" she said quietly. "The sun is shining on our right. We must be traveling north instead of south."

Her brother looked at the road signs, then consulted his map again. He groaned.

"You're right, Pam. We're going in the wrong direction."

"Oh, please find the way," begged Holly, "or we'll never get to the cameo factory in time!"

CHAPTER 16

A LITTLE GNARLED MAN

Worried at the delay, Mrs. Hollister parked by the side of the road. She and Pete pored over the map, trying to locate a simple route which would lead them south to Pompeii.

"Oh dear," the children's mother said finally, "we'll just have to plunge into Rome once more." As she spoke, a taxicab pulled alongside and stopped.

"Having trouble?" came the cheery voice of the cabbie.

"I'll say!" Pete called over to him.

The taxi man got out and stood beside the Hollisters' car. He was an Italian, he told them, who had worked for three years in Philadelphia.

"Then you can tell us how to get through Rome," Mrs. Hollister said hopefully.

"I'll take you," the cabbie offered. "Just follow me."

He hopped into his car and set off, with the Hollisters close behind. They went up and down street after street, with a crisscross here, a switchback there, around fountains, and along narrow one-way lanes. Finally they emerged in a broad avenue at the southern end of the city. The cabbie stopped by the roadside, leaned his head out the window and called to them, "Keep going straight ahead. You're okay now!"

"*Grazie!*" Pete said, grinning. "You saved us plenty of time!"

"Please let me pay you," the children's mother offered.

"No," the man replied. "It's my pleasure!"

As Mrs. Hollister protested, the cab driver turned about, and with a wave of his hand headed back into Rome.

"Aren't the Italians nice people?" Pam said as her mother drove along the broad highway. On either side the fields sloped gently up to the foot of green ridges. Here and there a little town snuggled on the mountain top, with slanting roofs circling a castle tower or a church spire.

"Isn't it romantic, Mother!" Pam exclaimed.

At noontime they stopped at a modern roadside restaurant before continuing their journey. Finally, a few miles north of Pompeii, they saw signs leading to the cameo factory.

A hundred yards off the main road lay the long low building made of white cement.

Mrs. Hollister drove to a parking lot beside it and everyone got out. They walked up to the main entrance, a large glass double door.

Pete pushed open one side for his mother and the others followed her into a large reception room. There they were greeted by a handsome middle-aged man wearing a dark jacket and a silk cravat. He had a long hooked nose, close-set brown eyes and dark hair brushed back in a flat pompadour.

"We're the Hollisters," Pete said, "and would like to see Mr. Caramagna."

"He cannot be disturbed," the man said without changing his expression.

"Oh!" Pam said. "Are you Mr. Nitto?"

"At your service, signorina," he said with a slight bow.

"We really must see Mr. Caramagna," the children's mother spoke up.

"About the robbery, I suppose."

"Yes."

Mr. Nitto lifted his chin and chuckled quietly. "Please do not talk about thieves," he said in a joking way. "It makes me nervous."

"How about us?" Holly asked. "We're nervous too, on account of your factory's going to be robbed!"

Mr. Nitto's smile vanished. With an annoyed look he said, "If I had to listen to the advice of children, I should soon be out of business."

"But the Roman police gave you the same warning," said Pete.

The secretary raised his eyebrows. "Naturally I couldn't tell them they were fools," he said, "but I thought so."

Pam, Pete and their mother pleaded with him to let them speak to Mr. Caramagna. But the secretary dismissed everything they said with a curt wave of his hands.

"Signor Caramagna is working," he said. Then he added with a smile, "Come. I will show you something interesting." He took them to the far end of the reception room, where they saw an exhibition booth. There, sitting at benches, were three men, bending over pieces of shell. Each worker had a small sharp knife, and was busily carving into the material.

"They are making cameos," Mr. Nitto said proudly. "The most beautiful ones in Italy."

One man was working on a lovely rosebud, the other two, carving heads of ladies with curly hair piled high.

The men looked up at the visitors, smiled, and continued at their jobs. Then the family was led into a heavily draped room. In the middle of the floor was a glass showcase and in it were cameos of exquisite beauty.

"They're breath-taking, aren't they?" Mrs. Hollister said to Pam.

"But the most beautiful is still to come," said Mr. Nitto. He told them that Mr. Caramagna would have his cameo of the First Lady finished that afternoon. "Please come back to see it."

"We're going to Pompeii now," Ricky said, "but we'll come here right afterward."

"I meant tomorrow," Mr. Nitto said, patting the boy on the head. "I'll tell Mr. Caramagna to expect you then."

As they climbed into their car again, Pete said, "I don't know what to make of Mr. Nitto. Sometimes he seems cold and other times friendly."

Pam was reluctant to drive on to Pompeii without notifying the local police of their hunch. "Maybe if we report the thieves' plan, they'll be on the lookout for them," she said.

Mrs. Hollister agreed and asked a passerby for directions to police headquarters. There, Pete told a lieutenant briefly about the impending robbery.

"*Sì, sì,*" the man answered with a patronizing smile. "Do not worry, little boy. We guard our town well. And after six o'clock at night we make regular checks on the cameo factory. It also has its own watchman and alarm system."

"Well," said Pete, when he had told the others, "we've done all in our power."

"Yes," his mother replied. "Maybe we're worrying too much."

"But if we locate the thieves I think we'll find Giovanni Boschi!" Pam insisted.

After getting a bite of lunch, they set off for Pompeii. Soon Ricky said, "Oh look, this is it. Here's a sign to the ruins."

Mrs. Hollister stopped the car in a large parking area. Other autos were pulling in and out, and tourists walking to or from the gateway to the ancient city.

Near the ticket booth Pete spied a Pulcinello show. He called to his brothers and sisters. "Look at this! It's something like ours at home!"

Punch, wearing a black and white checkered mask, stuck his head up and began to sing an Italian song in a high, piping voice.

"He's a funny one!" said Sue, reaching her arms up to Pete. Her brother picked her up and held her on his shoulders. Punch seemed to notice her. Thrusting his head forward he asked, *"Come si chiama?"*

"Sue!" the little girl cried out, and the bystanders laughed.

After Punch got whacked on the head by the devil, Mrs. Hollister said, "Come now, children, I have our tickets."

Pete reached up and turned Sue about and set her on the ground.

"I see that man," the little girl declared.

"What man?" Pete asked.

"The one by the lion's cage," she replied.

Pete followed her chubby, pointing finger and saw a man who looked like the sharp-faced fellow who had warned them in the Coliseum. He was talking to a small, misshapen man with bushy hair. A moment later the pair disappeared into the crowd, passing through the gateway.

Quickly Pete told the others what he had seen. "The gang is here!" he exclaimed. "That fellow is one of them."

"Pete, are you absolutely certain it's the same man we saw in Rome?" Mrs. Hollister asked.

"Well," her son replied, "I didn't get a good look

at his face last night, but I'm almost sure he's the one."

"I'm afraid this is the day the factory will be robbed," said Pam. "We'd better hurry back there."

"It's no use trying to warn them," said Holly, glumly.

"Anyhow he can't rob Caramagna as long as he's here," said Ricky.

"He probably came to spy on us," said Pete.

Ricky grinned. "Then we'll spy on him at the same time."

As the children went into the ancient city, they looked about but could not see the sharp-faced man and his companion.

Just then a handsome young guide stepped up to a knot of tourists and the Hollisters joined them. "Follow me," he said, "and I'll show you this famous old Greek seaport."

He led the sight-seers along a cobbled street, with two parallel ruts made by ancient chariot wheels. Several of the villas were intact, but in most cases only the walls remained standing.

The guide pointed out Mount Vesuvius in the distance. He told them that two thousand years before, ashes from the volcano had fallen upon the city, killing everyone.

"But being buried in ashes preserved these buildings," he explained. "Hundreds of years later the city was dug out."

Ricky tugged at Pam's arm.

"Don't do that," his sister said. "Listen to what the man is saying."

"Pam!" Ricky whispered. "Look at that funny guy!"

The girl turned about to see the man with the bushy hair peeking at them from behind a ruined stone wall. He ducked out of sight when he saw her spot him.

Pam signaled Pete, Holly and Ricky and they slipped away from the crowd for a quick conference. According to their plan, Ricky and Pete walked off casually, made a large circle behind the broken wall and came up in back of the fellow.

"Are you spying on us?" Ricky asked in a loud voice.

The gnarled man spun around and glared at the boys. Then he spoke a few words of Italian and limped off before Pete could question him.

"I don't think he speaks English," Ricky reported to the others.

"You've probably frightened the poor fellow," Mrs. Hollister said when they told her. "He might be just a visitor like us."

The tour of Pompeii lasted for over an hour. As the Hollisters looked at the remains of the forum and an ancient temple, they grew more and more uneasy. *Where were the sharp-faced man and his companion?* Both had vanished.

The guide told them that the sea, now some distance from the ruins, had once come up to the

"Are you spying on us?" Ricky asked.

very gates of the city. But Pete and Pam barely heard him, they were so worried.

"Maybe they're robbing the factory right this minute," Pete whispered to his mother.

She agreed. "The tour's nearly over," she said. "Let's go."

Although foot-weary and dusty after their long trek, the family ran back to their car. Mrs. Hollister tried to start it, but nothing happened.

"Oh no!" the children chorused.

Immediately suspicious, Pete jumped out, raised the hood and examined the motor.

"Just as I thought," he called. "Someone disconnected one of the wires!"

The boy put it back again. The motor started, Pete swung into his seat, and they headed for the cameo factory.

Mrs. Hollister made good time and soon was parking in the nearly empty lot beside the building. The family piled out and hurried to the front entrance.

A big sign in the doorway said, "Closed." Behind it, the drapes had been drawn across the glass doors.

As the others exchanged surprised looks, Sue got down flat on her tummy and peered beneath the bottom of the drape, which was an inch above the floor of the reception room.

"Ha-ha, I see something," Sue said gaily.

"What?" Pete whispered.

"There are lots of men in there and they're putting things in a sack!"

CHAPTER 17

THE BLUE GROTTO

"THE robbery!" Pete said hoarsely. "It's going on right now!"

Pam bent down to ask Sue exactly what she was seeing. She told her that all the men were wearing Punch false faces.

"This is terrible!" Mrs. Hollister said, glancing about for possible help.

Just then they heard a banging noise coming from one of the parked cars. Pete and Ricky ran over to find a man trussed and gagged in the back seat.

"It's Mr. Caramagna!" Pete called.

With Sue still watching the robbery, the other children and Mrs. Hollister untied the victim.

When the man had been released, they helped him to his feet.

"They're going now!" Sue called out. She got up and ran over to the others.

"They'll go out the back!" the cameo artist said. "Come, we must hurry!" But by the time they had raced across the parking lot to the rear of the building, the loud noise of motor scooters filled the air. Four riders zoomed past them, cut across the lot and sped down the road. Two of them had sacks over their shoulders.

As they roared along, Pete watched them fling the Punch masks aside. The disguises fell into the roadway.

"Let's chase them, Mother!" Pete said, running back toward the car.

"No, don't!" the factory owner called. He entered his factory by the back door, and the Americans followed. Inside, he telephoned to the police.

When he hung up, Pete said, "Mr. Caramagna, we tried to warn you about this robbery, but your secretary would not listen to us."

"Little wonder," the dejected artist said. "Nitto was the one responsible for the whole thing." He flung up his hands and continued, "I should never have hired that man, but he had such a smooth way about him."

The factory owner walked dejectedly up to his showcase. He pointed to the open glass lids and sighed. "Thousands of dollars worth of antique cameos—gone! And the 'First Lady,' the beautiful carving I just made! It has been stolen, too!"

"The President will be disappointed," Holly said.

While they were waiting for the police to arrive, Mr. Caramagna told how Nitto had planned the theft. The secretary had dismissed the workmen early that afternoon. Then, shortly after the artist had placed his newly made cameo in the case, Nitto admitted the thieves and ordered them to tie the factory owner up. "He bragged to me that he'd be

164

out of Italy before I could catch him," Mr. Caramagna said, "but we shall see!"

Pete and Pam paced about, impatient for the police to arrive. If Nitto were going to flee the country, he would probably take Giovanni Boschi with him.

"Oh, that poor man!" Mrs. Hollister said. As she spoke, they heard the police cars outside. The officers hurried in and Italian words flew back and forth as the factory owner told what had happened.

"The Hollister children warned you. Why did you not listen?" he asked them.

The police were embarrassed, but said they had no way of knowing Nitto would pull an inside job.

After hearing the whole story, the officers left quickly in search of the fugitives. They stopped only long enough to pick up the Punch masks, which they hoped would provide a clue to the scoundrels.

Meanwhile, Pete and Pam continued to ply Mr. Caramagna with questions about Nitto. The fellow, they learned, had often said he would like to go to South America.

"That's where he'll probably head for now," Pete reasoned. "We must hurry if we want to catch him."

"What were his habits?" Pam asked. "What did he do in his spare time?"

The cameo artist said that his secretary was very much interested in art work. "He would travel all over Italy admiring painting and sculpture."

"Glassware, too?" Pam asked.

"Yes, that also was one of his hobbies," Signor Caramagna replied.

"Where did Mr. Nitto spend his weekends?" Pam wanted to know.

"On the island of Capri," replied the factory owner promptly. "He went often—said he liked the view."

"Then let's go there and see if we can find him," Holly piped up.

Pete agreed. He reasoned that the gang's headquarters might be on Capri. "If Giovanni and the loot are still hidden there, the gang will have to stop to pick them up. It's worth a chance," he added.

"I like your courage," the crestfallen artist said with a wan smile. "Besides, Capri is one place you should see before leaving Italy."

The man suggested that they put up for the night at Sorrento. "Then tomorrow morning you can take the boat to the island. Be sure to visit the Blue Grotto."

"What kind of an animal is that, Mommy?" asked Sue. She was told that the Blue Grotto was a special kind of cave.

"You'll see," her mother promised.

The Hollisters took their leave of the sad artist. But before they left, the children's mother said, "If my brother-in-law Russ Hollister gets in touch with you, please tell him where we'll be."

An hour later, the family was driving along the rocky coast of southern Italy. The narrow road wove in and out around cliffs, with the beautiful sea stretching far to the west below them. Finally they came to Sorrento, a lovely resort town, nestled at the top of a steep precipice.

After finding a hotel, the Hollisters had dinner, then wandered about a delightful square until bedtime. Although they had kept watch for the gang, they had seen none of them.

Next morning the family climbed down a long flight of stairs to the beach. With other tourists they boarded a boat and started across the water for Capri. Ahead of them lay the towering island, blue-gray, in the hazy morning sunlight. At the foot of a sheer rock wall was a huddle of rowboats.

"That's the grotto," said a man sitting near Pete. "We'll stop there for a while."

The passenger vessel drew close and rode at anchor on the swelling sea while the rowboats pulled alongside and the tourists got in.

The oarsmen were dressed in colorful shirts and rolled-up trousers. Each stood in the middle of his boat while two passengers sat in front, two in back. Mrs. Hollister and the girls went into one craft. Pete and Ricky stepped down into the next one with two other passengers.

The boys admired the skill of their oarsman as he guided them to a gaping hole in the rock wall. Then, shipping oars, the boatman grabbed a chain at the mouth of the cave. "Down, everybody!" he cried. The boys flattened themselves on the bottom. The oarsman bent back and gave a mighty pull, propelling the craft into a vast vault of the cave.

"Ooooh, it's dark in here!" came Holly's voice

Ahead was the rock wall.

from somewhere ahead of them. In a few seconds everyone's eyes became accustomed to the gloom. Then they saw the marvelous color. The watery floor of the cave glistened sapphire blue from the sunlight sifting in from the base of the cliff.

"I love the Blue Grotto!" Sue cried out gleefully.

The boatmen rowed around the cave several times. Then one by one the little crafts headed for the opening. There they waited for the bottom of a swell and *whiz!* They were shot out into the sunshine!

Once the sight-seers were back on the passenger boat, it cruised along the rocky shore, finally coming to a tiny harbor. The Hollisters debarked with the rest of the people and made their way across a long wharf to where small buses awaited them.

The children's mother suggested that they visit Anacapri first, a small town atop the rocky island. The buses, seating only ten passengers, were narrow and had no tops.

"Yikes!" Ricky said. "They look like little fire engines."

When everyone was seated, the driver adjusted his sunglasses and took off up a steep, narrow road which wound like a tiny ribbon higher and higher up the cliff wall.

The turns were steep and sharp, and before each one the driver honked his horn to warn any car which might be coming from the opposite direction.

Halfway to the top, while the youngsters gazed out over the sea toward Sorrento, the brakes suddenly squealed and the bus jerked to a stop. Before them, coming around the curve, was another car. It stopped only inches from them.

Pete, sitting in the front, craned forward and looked at the passengers in the rear seat of the small car. One was Olevi, the thief from Venice; the other, the gnarled little man from Pompeii.

CHAPTER 18

THE MYSTERIOUS TOWER

"Stop! Halt!" Pete cried out to the occupants of the car as it started to back up.

"We must catch those men!" Ricky cried out.

The thieves backed farther to a wider part of the road, turned about and sped up the hill toward Anacapri.

The bus driver regarded the excited Hollisters skeptically, shrugged and set off once more. By the time the narrow, curving highway brought them to Anacapri, the rascals were nowhere to be seen.

The family alighted at the summit of the rocky island, where souvenir shops, restaurants, and several small hotels sat like a topknot on Capri. Through the haze in the distance loomed Vesuvius, and far below, tiny boats plied the shimmering blue sea. But the Hollisters had no time for scenery.

"Mother," Pete suggested, "suppose you stay here near the road just in case the thieves try to escape in their car."

"What are you going to do?" Mrs. Hollister asked.

Pete suggested that he and Ricky work as a team and Pam and Holly do the same.

"We'll look all around the place and see if we can spy any of those crooks," Pete declared.

"All right, but don't be too long," their mother replied. "Sue and I will wait here for you."

The girls set off in one direction, Pete and Ricky in another. The two boys peered into curio shops, poked their heads into restaurants and mingled with the crowd of sight-seers hoping to spot the faces of the fugitives. No luck. Then the brothers scrambled over a stony field, finally stopping beneath an umbrella pine tree.

Between them and the edge of the cliff were several villas. One, with a square tower rising above the terra-cotta roofs, seemed to be deserted. Boards were nailed across the tightly shuttered windows.

As Pete was wondering whether to make inquiries at the other houses, he noticed a man's head bobbing in the tall grass near the villa with the tower.

"Ricky, look at that!" The figure bent low and hastened through scrubby brush and boulders near the cliff's edge.

"Yikes! That's the little guy we saw at Pompeii."

"Come on—after him!"

The two boys ran toward the cliff, but when they were halfway to the mysterious little man they stopped in wonderment. The fellow had parted the tall grass and was beckoning to them!

"This may be a trap."

"Wait a minute," Pete cautioned. "This may be a trap."

"I wonder what he wants," said Ricky. "Don't you think we should find out?"

The brothers advanced cautiously. The little man dropped out of sight for a moment. Then his eyes peered above the grass again.

"Maybe he's going to try to throw us into the sea," Ricky said, and the boys walked more slowly.

Pete cupped his hands. "What do you want?" he called out.

"He won't understand you," Ricky said. "Remember, he doesn't speak English."

With that, the gnarled fellow called back, "I want to talk to you."

"See!" Pete said. "He *does* speak English."

As the brothers stepped forward the man backed into the shade of a huge rock only a few feet from the rim of the cliff. Pete and Ricky approached him, prepared to spring to safety at any moment.

"What do you want?" Pete asked again.

The little man had a pained expression on his face. His eyes were full of fright. "Go away. Go home. Hurry," he said. "You are in great danger. My brother will hurt you."

"Your brother?" Pete asked. "Who's he?"

"Nitto. He will not allow you to spoil his plans. I tell you, he is a bad man. Go, now, while you are able to."

Pete spoke up boldly. "Is Nitto holding Giovanni Boschi?"

The question hit the wizened man like an electric shock. He jumped, looked wildly about, then dashed off with the speed of a weasel.

Pete and Ricky set after him, and with a flying dive the older boy brought the fellow to the ground. But he wriggled and thrashed about with such vigor that he escaped from Pete's grasp. He scooted off among a pile of boulders and was out of sight.

As Pete picked himself off the ground, Ricky said, "I tried to grab him, but he got away."

Instead of chasing the little man, the two slid behind a tall rock. "We'll wait," Pete said. "If he's hiding, he's bound to come out soon. Then we'll follow him."

Ten minutes went by; fifteen, twenty. Finally the boys' patience paid off. They saw a head emerge from the crags. The little man, crouching lower than ever, slipped off in the direction of the shuttered villa.

Quietly, Pete and Ricky followed, ducking behind rocks and bushes.

Finally the boys dived into the tall grass and observed Nitto's brother opening the back door of the villa. He slipped in, and they heard a bolt click shut.

"Come on, Ricky," Pete said. "Let's get in there somehow and find out what's going on."

"We've been gone a long time," his brother whispered. "Mother will be worried about us."

"There's no time to lose," Pete replied. "That fellow was trying to frighten us off."

"I don't think he's a bad man," Ricky said. "Maybe he was trying to help us."

Pete looked up at the tower. "Do you suppose Giovanni Boschi—"

Just then they heard the bolt click again. The door opened, and the gnarled fellow came out. He had a coil of rope over one shoulder, and made directly for the cliff's edge.

"Now's our chance," Pete whispered when the fellow was out of sight. The two boys got up and ran to the villa, entered the half-open door and stepped inside. They found themselves in a long cool hallway. Men's voices were coming from somewhere at the far end. Pete held his finger to his lips and they tiptoed up to the last room. Sounds of a hot argument came right through the closed door.

"That's Nitto's voice, all right," Pete whispered into his brother's ear.

"I'll bet they're fighting over the loot," Ricky replied softly.

Suddenly the brothers froze with excitement as the words "Giovanni Boschi" came to their ears.

"They're arguing about him!" Pete said. "Ricky, he must be right here in this villa!"

The two glanced about, and saw a stairway leading upward.

Pressing close to the wall to keep the boards from creaking, Pete led the way. The boys climbed two flights, then started up the narrow steps into the dim tower. At the top they came to a heavy wooden door. Beside it on a wall hook was a large brass key. While Ricky listened nervously for footsteps coming up, Pete fitted the key in the lock and quietly opened the door.

Cautiously they walked into a small, gloomy room with only a little skylight in the ceiling. As their eyes grew accustomed to the dimness, Pete and Ricky spied a wooden table. Seated at it was a white-haired man. He looked at the boys with glazed eyes.

"Giovanni Boschi? Is that you?" Pete asked.

Fearful, the old fellow raised his arms as if to ward off a blow.

"We won't hurt you," Ricky said. "We're friends of Nada."

The puppeteer blinked. "How can I believe you?" he asked.

Quickly, Pete pulled the tiny puppet head from his pocket. "Nada gave us this," he said. "Do you believe me now?"

Giovanni's face lighted up.

"Yes, yes," he said eagerly, then in a pleading voice added, "Please get me out of here. They're going to take me to South America."

"Come with us right now," said Pete. "Hurry!" As the old man stood up, hurried footsteps pounded on the stairs. The door burst open. There stood Nitto!

"Who let you in here?" the thief thundered.

Although Ricky quaked with fright he managed to say, "Your brother left the door open."

"How do you know my brother?" the man stormed, and strode across the room toward the two boys. Just then light steps sounded on the steps and Nitto wheeled about. "Gino!" he shouted. "I'll—"

The thief's face turned purple with rage as he saw a uniformed policeman blocking the doorway. Several more pushed into the room and quickly snapped handcuffs on the surprised robber.

Another policeman escorted Giovanni Boschi and the boys downstairs. It seemed as if the whole house were filled with officers and plainclothesmen. Ricky and Pete were open-mouthed at the speed with which the shuttered villa was raided.

As they stepped out the front door, Giovanni Boschi stopped short. As he stood blinking in the sunlight, the girls and Mrs. Hollister hurried up to greet them.

"Yikes!" Ricky exclaimed. "What's going on?"

While Pam, Holly and Sue helped the old man to a bench in the shade of a tree, Mrs. Hollister explained to her sons that when they had not returned, she had sent the two girls to look for them. They had seen their brothers enter the abandoned villa, observed Gino return and close the door, then had raced back to tell their mother. She spread the alarm at once and the police closed in quickly.

"Yikes, thanks, Mother!" said Ricky.

"That was great teamwork," Pete agreed.

By this time five prisoners, including Nitto, stood in a line before the villa as the police interrogated them in Italian.

First was Nitto, his face still flushed with anger. Beside him drooped the small man with the mustache. Next came long-haired Olevi and the sharp-faced Neapolitan. At the end stood poor Gino, who had tried to warn Pete and Ricky away.

Meanwhile four officers carried the stolen treasure from the house. First came the glass Madonna, then the painting, the statue, and, finally, the First Lady cameo.

"Won't Mr. Caramagna be glad to see that!" Pete exclaimed.

"And don't forget Uncle Russ," Holly said.

"I, too, owe you thanks," declared Giovanni Boschi, and told them his strange story. As Pete had guessed, the puppeteer had overheard the thieves making plans as he set up his booth in a park in Milan. All were there except Gino. "They were on the other side of some bushes," the showman said. "When they saw me, I ran to my motorcycle and headed out of town. But they caught me."

"How did you ever manage to leave the *aiuto* note?" asked Pam.

The old man smiled. "The men threw me into their car and I pretended to be dazed. While they stood around my cycle, arguing what to do with it, I wrote the message, stuck it in the Punch head and tossed it out the window."

179

"Then where did the bad men take you?" asked Sue.

"Venice," he replied, "and there I got away from them twice."

"To buy the postcard and again to mail it," guessed Pete.

"Yes. Then Olevi stayed in Venice and the others took me to Rome. There I was blindfolded and had a long ride in a car and finally by boat. I couldn't see out of my prison," the old fellow added, "so I never did know where I was."

When questioned about the Punch puppets that had appeared for sale, Giovanni said, "That's where Gino made a mistake." The showman had convinced his gnarled jailer that he could make money by selling Pulcinellos. "He brought me materials and I made them in the tower. When Nitto found out, he put a stop to it," the puppeteer said, "but Rocco had already sold some."

Pete pointed to the sharp-faced thief. "That man, you mean?"

Giovanni Boschi looked at the boy in amazement.

"He's from Naples, isn't he?" Pete added.

"Yes, how did you know?"

Holly grinned. "Just wait, Mr. Boschi, we have oodles to tell you!"

"Why did the gang want to take you to South America?" Pam asked, puzzled. "Once they'd escaped, what would it matter if you told on them?"

"I had heard too much," said the old man. "Nitto

also has henchmen in Brazil. I know where their headquarters are and what places he planned to rob."

As he spoke, the prisoners were led past to a waiting van. Nitto wheeled about and glared at the Hollisters. "Why did you ever have to come to Italy?" he cried out. "All was going well until then."

"It wasn't going well for Giovanni Boschi," Pete spoke up.

"You should be ashamed of kidnaping this nice man," Pam chided him.

"I'd like to ask Mr. Nitto a few questions," Pete told the officer and received permission.

"What was your brother's part in this?" Pete asked the gang leader.

"He was only Boschi's jailer," Nitto replied scornfully, "and did odd jobs."

"Where was he going with that rope?" asked Ricky.

Nitto looked pained. "When Olevi came rushing in and said he and Gino'd seen you Hollisters coming up in the bus, I told my brother to hang a rope down the cliff so we could escape that way if necessary. We argued about it because the others thought it was too dangerous to take the old man."

"Gino tried to help us by warning us," Pete told the officer.

"He wasn't as bad as the rest," Ricky put in.

"No doubt he will get off more lightly," the policeman assured them.

Pete turned again to Nitto. "How did you know that we were in Milan?" the boy asked.

The thief said that he had been prowling outside Nada's apartment to learn the best way to steal the passport. The door had been ajar and he heard the girl answer Pam's telephone call. "I didn't want anyone to interfere with my plans," he said, "so I phoned one of my men in Milan and ordered him to warn you."

After the Hollisters left Milan, they had been only a step behind the thieves all the way.

Nitto admitted it was he who answered the phone and posed as Nada's father the day he had stolen the passport.

"We tried to scare you off," Nitto said. "Yesterday I was afraid you would come back to the factory, so I had Rocco and Gino disconnect the wires in your car. But even that didn't stop you." Then he hung his head. "I never have seen such detectives!"

With all the answers finally wrung from the gang leader, the police led him over to his four crestfallen henchmen waiting at the van. As they did, another car pulled up. Out stepped Uncle Russ and Signor Caramagna.

"So you've done it again!" the cartoonist said with a big grin, and embraced the youngsters, who flocked about him.

The police handed the artist his finished cameo

and Pam said with a smile, "Now everybody's happy."

"All except them," Ricky said, pointing at the prisoners as they were loaded into the police van.

The last one in line, Nitto, hesitated before getting in. One of the policemen prodded the hook-nosed man with a small club.

"Poor Punch!" Sue declared. "He's losing again!"